"Like the way I chose to take the blame for the fire when the deputy came to question me," Rio said. "I knew the consequences, Meg, but I did it because I wanted to protect you. I loved you."

An acrid thickness welled up inside Meg's chest, pushing tears into her throat, her eyes. She took a deep breath, holding on by the fingernails she dug into her palms. "I appreciate that, Rio. Really, I do. But I wish you'd told them the truth."

"I didn't know the truth," he said quietly. "You were gone."

Dear Reader,

In *Cowboy Comes Home,* the hero and heroine both return to Wyoming after many years away. So have I—fictionally speaking. Eight years ago, I wrote my very first Harlequin Superromance, *The Maverick,* with the small-town setting of Treetop, Wyoming. A good creation never dies—at least in my imagination—so when I decided to write a story featuring a reformed bad girl, a cowboy hero and a ranch named Wild River, I knew I had to return to Treetop.

To refresh my memory, I revisited *The Maverick* for the first time since it was published. Fun research. (Though slightly scary, since it was way too late to revise!) Then I reread parts of Mary O'Hara's Wyoming-set "Flicka" series, which are among my favorite books from my horse-crazy years. Even more fun. Sometimes being a writer is the best job in the world.

I hope you enjoy this Wyoming reunion story. *Cowboy Comes Home* is my ninth Harlequin Superromance book—with more to come. And it all started in Treetop....

Happy reading,

Carrie Alexander

P.S. Visit me on the Web at www.carriealexander.com, where you can also find my backlist and drop me a line.

Cowboy Comes Home
Carrie Alexander

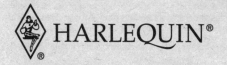

TORONTO • NEW YORK • LONDON
AMSTERDAM • PARIS • SYDNEY • HAMBURG
STOCKHOLM • ATHENS • TOKYO • MILAN • MADRID
PRAGUE • WARSAW • BUDAPEST • AUCKLAND

Recycling programs
for this product may
not exist in your area.

ISBN-13: 978-0-373-71614-2

COWBOY COMES HOME

www.eHarlequin.com

Printed in U.S.A.

ABOUT THE AUTHOR

Carrie Alexander lives and writes among the birches and pine trees in Upper Michigan, where she enjoys gardening (sporadically), swimming (when it's warm enough), collecting sticks and stones (they breed in her yard), and waiting for football season (Go Pack!).

Books by Carrie Alexander

HARLEQUIN SUPERROMANCE

*North Country Stories

Don't miss any of our special offers. Write to us at the following address for information on our newest releases.

Harlequin Reader Service
U.S.: 3010 Walden Ave., P.O. Box 1325, Buffalo, NY 14269
Canadian: P.O. Box 609, Fort Erie, Ont. L2A 5X3

CHAPTER ONE

MEG LENNOX HELD OUT one hand, offering a palmful of sweet feed to the balky gelding showing her his hindquarters. Behind her back she clutched the rope attached to the halter hung off her shoulder. The way the horse had reacted to her previous attempts to catch him, she might as well have been throwing a rattlesnake around his neck.

The chestnut lashed his tail. He wasn't easily fooled.

"Quiet now." She chirruped, shaking her palm like a gambler with hot dice. "Don't you want your dinner?"

Sloop's ears flicked back and forth. His head turned as if he might be persuaded, but the one visible eye rolled with suspicion, showing a white rim.

She stood still, even though the temptation to sidle closer was strong. The horse was almost within touching distance, the closest she'd come to catching him during their half-hour battle of wills.

"Hey, Sloop. Good fella. There's nothing to be afraid of. Don't run away."

Don't run away? The words pinched Meg's conscience. She'd always been good at running away.

She gazed past the fence and the weather-worn barn

to the rolling pastures of Wild River Ranch. It was early October in Treetop, Wyoming, and the rich grassy greens of summer had faded to tan and ochre. The upright stands of high-country aspen marched up the foothills in golden epaulets.

She'd loved the ranch, but not her life here. Ten years ago, at barely eighteen, she'd left behind her home and contentious relationship with her gruff, uncaring father. Forever, she'd thought.

But in all the years she'd searched, she hadn't been able to find the good life she'd expected. When times had gotten really tough, she'd instinctively fled back to Wyoming. To the ranch. Even though it hadn't been home for a long time, even in her heart.

Especially in her heart.

Meg turned her sigh into another crooning overture to Sloop. Some days, her hopes for the ranch—and herself—seemed as unattainable as the stubborn gelding.

She'd returned too late. Both parents were dead, the land neglected. Her prospects were as bleak as the metallic-gray sky.

But I'm home at last, even if it's only half a home. That's something.

She chirruped again. "Sloop. Please let me catch you. It's gonna rain."

The horse didn't mind being out in the rain, but she hadn't hammered and nailed the box stalls into shape for her own amusement. Renny and Caprice were already inside, pulling at the hay nets, their grain long gone. Only Sloop was being stubborn. His owner had warned her that the horse could be hard to catch. Meg had been certain she'd have no trouble. Once upon a time, she'd had a reputation for being good with horses.

Sloop swung around, his nostrils fluttering. The delayed dinnertime was finally getting to him.

She opened her hand. The feed was moist and fragrant in her palm. "There you go," she soothed him. "One more step and you're mine, you ornery old rat-tailed nag."

Ears twitching, the horse extended his nose to inhale the grain. She raised her other hand to his neck, sliding the halter rope across his flaxen mane.

She was just reaching around to catch it into a loose lasso when a truck burst around the bend, frame rattling, gears grinding. The flock of starlings that had been pecking along the fence line rose suddenly. Sloop flung up his head and wheeled away with a snort.

Meg threw the halter on the ground. "Dammit!"

She strode to the fence, calling a surly "What do you want?" at the driver of the pickup truck.

The door opened. A man stepped out. "Is that any way to greet an old friend?"

Meg stopped with one leg slung over the top railing. Everything inside her had seized into one tight, hard lump. Her shock felt an awful lot like pain.

The voice was deeper, rougher. But she recognized it, even if the face and physique were a stranger's.

Rio Carefoot.

Her first love. The boy whose life she'd carelessly ruined on the night she ran away.

The man she'd most dreaded facing up to, even ahead of her dad.

Meg dropped back down into the dirt, keeping the fence between them. As if Rio had any chance of getting close to her. She'd wrapped barbed wire around her heart.

"Rio," she said flatly. "You're not supposed to be in Treetop."

"Neither are you."

"I've been back since July."

"Three days for me."

Meg grabbed the fence rail to steady herself. She didn't want Rio to know how badly she was thrown. "What brings you here?"

He glanced away. "My mother's still around."

She understood the underlying implication. "Around" meant living in as a housekeeper for William Walker Stone on his multimillion-dollar spread east of town. Any Treetopper asked would have said that Rio returning to the Stone ranch was about as likely as Meg coming back to her father's place.

Well, look at them now. There must be some fine skating in hell.

"I heard that," she said. He was glowering. Still holding a grudge? "But I meant *here.* Wild River."

"You wrote an ad. Help Wanted."

The classified ad for a stablehand had been running

in the *Treetop Weekly* for the past month. She'd had two applicants, a kid who could only work after school, and the town drunk who had a history of holding odd jobs only long enough to fund his next bender. She'd taken the kid's number.

Rio rested his hands on his hips, face turned to follow Sloop, who was prancing at the far end of the pasture. Rio wore jeans and a chambray shirt beneath a new-looking leather jacket lined in fleece. The black hair she'd once braided down his back barely reached his collar. He'd filled out some during the past decade, but the weight was all broad shoulders and lean, hard muscle. He'd be twenty-nine now. One year older than herself. Only one, yet even when they were kids he'd been the wiser and nobler one. He'd already known that love could mean sacrifice.

She still hadn't looked into his eyes. Her gaze was fixed somewhere near his left shoulder.

Rio's Adam's apple bobbed. "Room and board, the ad said, plus a small salary."

"You're applying for the job?"

"You're shocked."

"What—" She bit the inside of her lip. "My dad passed away. It's just me here now."

"So I heard."

"Right. Even though I swore I'd never return." With all the fervor of a hot-blooded teenager who had no idea of how rough life could really get.

Rio's eyes narrowed. "Why did you?"

"I had nowhere else to go," she said before she could stop herself. Rio didn't have to know that she'd retreated here, a failure. If he realized how barren her life had become, he might get the idea that she was looking for more than help with the horses.

He nodded perfunctorily. "I know what that's like."

Meg could sympathize. While her dad had been a hard, emotionless man with no idea how to raise a daughter, Rio's father had never even acknowledged him. Of course he'd understand what it felt like to be homeless. *Her* estrangement had been her own choice.

She cleared her throat, hoping to keep the shakiness out of her voice. "You've been in the army all this time."

"Yeah. Until five weeks ago."

He'd been deployed to heavy action in Afghanistan several times, she'd heard around town. There were old acquaintances eager to fill her in. Stop-lossed the last time, they'd said, called back to action just when he'd thought he was out for good. His mother had been devastated.

Meg's eyes squeezed shut. *My fault.*

She certainly owed him a job, at the least. Why he'd want work as a stable hand was a mystery she'd have to consider later. Right now, the prospect of having Rio live on the ranch with her was almost incomprehensible. Only in a small, hidden place deep inside had she ever considered seeing him again. Making it up to him.

She wasn't ready for any of that.

"I don't think it's going to work out," she said. The part-time kid would have to do.

Rio didn't question her. He moved along the fence. Sloop had stopped showing off and was watching them with his head hung low, his ribs bellowing. The bucket of grain she'd been using to lure him was parked nearby.

"How many horses?" Rio asked.

"Just three." Her training and boarding business wasn't off to a flying start. "But I've got two more coming to board for the winter—" *maybe* "—and I thought I'd pick up a few green prospects at the fall auction in Laramie. Work with them through the winter, sell for a profit in the spring."

Rio shed his jacket. "Make you a bet."

"What?" Once she'd have taken up any challenge, but she'd lived in Vegas the past six years. Wagering was a losing game.

"If I can get that horse into the barn within ten minutes, you'll hire me on a trial basis." He didn't wait for her assent, just climbed the fence and picked up the bucket and the halter. He coiled the rope neatly, watching her out of the corner of his eye. Much like the stubborn chestnut, except his whites barely showed.

Rio had dark eyes, a deep midnight blue that was nearly black. Her reflection in them used to make her feel beautiful, though the girl she'd seen in the mirror had been anything but.

Meg looked at her grimy hands. She wiped them on her equally grimy sweatshirt. "His name's Sloop."

Rio didn't play coy. He walked directly to the gelding, cutting a swath through the fawn-colored field. She heard him murmuring—a soft, velvety sound that brought back memories of teenage trysts in the tight, enclosed space of his pickup truck. Lying together in the cool grass by the river. Their bodies tangled and wet in the hot golden light of the haymow.

She closed her eyes. They'd been sixteen and seventeen. Too young to know that they were playing with fire.

"Sloop," Rio said softly, making her look again. He might as well have said *sweet,* the way he used to when he kissed her.

The horse's ears were on a swivel, flicking back and forth. He'd thrown up his head. His flanks quivered as Rio approached. But he didn't move.

Rio held out the bucket. Sloop lunged for it. The halter went on so fast the feat seemed almost a sleight of hand.

"That was no fair," Meg called. "I wore him down for you."

Rio's sandpaper chuckle drifted across the pasture. "You ought to know, Meggie Jo. All's fair in love and war."

She flinched. She hadn't been called Meggie Jo in a very long time. Only her mom and Rio had been allowed to use the nickname, though her father had often said *Margaret Jolene Lennox* in his most forbidding tone, when he'd been calling her to his study for another dressing down.

Rio rubbed a hand along the horse's neck, giving Sloop a moment with the grain before he took the bucket. Meg got her emotions in check and went to push the corral gate open wider, then the Dutch door to the box stall, even though both were already ajar.

Rio, living on her ranch. That couldn't possibly work.

But why not? First she could make it clear that she wasn't looking for any sort of romantic reunion, and then she could make amends. If that even mattered anymore, so many years after she'd made a wreck of both their lives.

Rio led Sloop into the stall. The horse was docile now that he'd been caught, nickering hello to his stablemates, then nudging his nose at Meg to prod her into fetching his feed.

She ran her hand along the gelding's flank, moving slowly only because Rio stood on the horse's other side and suddenly the stall seemed smaller than before.

He looked at her over the chestnut's withers. "Flashy horse. Registered?"

"AQHA." American Quarter Horse Association. "Bonny Bar's Windrunner, which somehow got translated into the stable name Sloop. He belongs to a woman from town. She's a beginner, but she hopes to show him next summer. I'm going to work with them till then."

"Look at me, Meg."

Her throat ached. "I can't."

"I'm only me."

"It's been ten years and then some."

"We've both changed. But I still know you. You know me, too."

She met his eyes. A searing heat sliced through her, the arc of a flaming arrow. She pictured Rio, bare chested, bronzed and beautiful as he pulled back the bowstring.

She forced out the words. "That's why it won't work."

"Or why it will."

She was afraid of that, too.

"Why do you want this job? It's nothing. Not challenging or rewarding. Hardly any pay. And isolated."

"Exactly what I'm looking for. See, it's the room and board that's valuable to me. I can do the work easily and still have time for…other things."

"Like what?"

The horse shifted between them, curving his neck around to nuzzle at Meg.

"That's personal," Rio said.

She eyed him.

"Nothing sinister," he said. "Just a project I'm working on."

"All right, if that's the way you want it." She ducked beneath Sloop's neck and took the bucket from Rio. His fingers brushed against hers, but she jerked away, trying to make it look as though she'd only been moving toward the stall door. She went to the feed bins and dipped out a couple of scoops, then returned to tip the bucket into Sloop's feed pan.

Rio was already filling the hay net. "Give me a week," he said. "A trial."

Her head snapped back. *Trial.* He'd used the word twice now. On purpose? To remind her what she owed him, after almost putting him on trial for a crime he hadn't committed?

She secured the bottom half of the Dutch door. No, Rio wouldn't taunt her with the past. Her guilty conscience was talking again, a voice she'd managed to drown out for the past ten years with a loud life that had ultimately said nothing at all.

At Wild River, the silence spoke. Too loudly. She'd be grateful to have another person around. They might even be able to reestablish their old friendship.

But never their status as lovers. Never.

"I'll show you the bunkhouse," she said abruptly. "You might change your mind."

RIO REMEMBERED the bunkhouse. Even back then the one-room cabin had been run down, as dark as a cave. The Lennoxes had had a hired man, an old cowboy named Rooney. He'd chewed tobacco, tied flies that never caught fish, kept a string of sleazy paperbacks in his back pocket that he'd read in the barn in between chores. Meg had been the bane of his existence, with her mischief making and harum-scarum horseback riding.

Rio lifted the limp curtain that hung at the cabin's only window. The view was of the river that cut through the property, deep, black and turbulent. Rooney had fished there, futilely. Rio and Meg had shot the rapids on their backsides.

"Do you remember the time you put cayenne pepper into Rooney's tobacco tin?"

Meg almost smiled. "He's dead now." She bent over a small square table, wiping a thick layer of dust with her sleeve. "He's dead, too," she added to herself.

"He must have been seventy when I knew him." Rio tried the lamp. "There's electricity." He crossed to the bathroom, outfitted with a rust-spotted claw-foot tub and cast-iron sink. The pipes clattered before blatting a brown stream into the bowl. "And water."

Meg had pried a book from beneath the table leg. The table wobbled when she dropped the curled paperback on top of it. "The place needs work. I'll clean it out and get a new mattress. Set some mousetraps."

Rio moved over to examine the faded cover of the book. A buxom blonde with a gun winked up at him. *Jezebel's Revenge.* Cover price forty-five cents.

"Are you saying I have the job?"

"If you want it."

"I want it."

She let out a breath, clearly exasperated with him. "Have you turned crazy in your old age, Rio Carefoot?"

He'd been crazy for her. Crazy for a green-eyed girl with rebellion streaming through her veins. The Meg of his youth hadn't given a flying fig that he was a rootless outsider, halfway Crow, who'd never had a home of his own.

No real father either. But there'd always been his mother, who'd wanted him only to be good and get along. Virginia Carefoot hadn't approved of her son's fatal-attraction friendship with Meg, but after sending him away to one failed summer at the Montana rez with his grandparents, she'd run out of ways to keep them apart.

"What about you?" he asked Meg abruptly, not willing to acknowledge that, for him, the attraction hadn't faded. She was still a part of him, even though he'd been sure he'd never see her again. "Where have you been all this time?"

"Around." She circled the room, poking at the secondhand furnishings, as restive and uneasy as the young Meg. "Vegas, mostly. I arrived on the back of a motorcycle and left in a thirdhand Camaro with bad brakes, so you can guess how well I did there." She rubbed her palms, drawing his eyes to the tattoos encircling her wrists. On the right, a ring of flame. The left, a blue band of waves.

"What did you do there?"

She pulled at her sleeves. "A little bit of everything— waitressing, clerking, answering phones at a call center. Pink-ghetto jobs. Then for nearly two years, I was on the city crew that did nothing but change lightbulbs. It was nice to be outdoors."

"Huh. And how many *does* it take to change a lightbulb?"

She rolled her eyes. "You're not the first to ask that eternal question. The guys' standard answer was that now that they had a woman on the crew, the screwing had become a spectator sport. They were a rowdy bunch."

Rio wanted to leap to her defense, even now. "You should have found a new job."

"Eventually I did. There was some trouble and I was let go. So long, cushy city benefits." Shadows shuttered the expression on her downturned face. "My dad always said I'd amount to nothing."

"But he left you the ranch."

"No one else wanted it. If he'd ever had friends, he'd chased them away long before he died."

"Were you here at the end?"

She nodded behind a curtain of hair. "I came home. A neighbor—Mrs….um…Mrs. Vaughn—she tracked me down off a Christmas card I'd sent the old man. But he didn't want me. He told me to leave, to come back only after he was six feet deep."

Rio looked at her, the bed between them. He'd have liked to go to her, but again he stopped himself. Even the young Meg had been prickly about accepting affection. This Meg had Hands Off branded across every inch of her.

"That was three years ago." She brushed her hair over her shoulders. It was the same—long and straight, the color of pecans dipped in taffy. With her slim body and tawny skin, she'd always been camouflaged, easy to lose among the tall reeds and saplings of their endless summers. But she'd been free-spirited then. Now her camouflage seemed like the stillness of a wild creature frightened of capture.

Rio gave a soft grunt. "Don't worry. We'll set the old place to rights."

Meg had moved to the door they'd left standing open. "I want this clear from the start—there is no 'we.' That's over. I'm not looking for…you know. I don't need a partner. You'd be just the hired hand."

He gazed at her. "Of course."

Her wide mouth pulled taut. "I'm sorry if that was harsh."

"No, it's good to know where we stand. This is only a job for me."

"Then we're clear." Her eyes darkened despite what she'd said.

"Clear enough for now."

"I mean it, Rio. I'm done with men."

He followed her out the door. She'd always been a man's woman. Never interested in girlie things when there were horses to ride, fast cars to drive, dares to take.

But someone had hurt her badly.

He hoped it wasn't him.

CHAPTER TWO

As SOON AS the rattle of Rio's retreating truck had died, Meg slammed into the house. Tears welled in her eyes. She dashed them away impatiently. She didn't cry.

But, oh, sometimes she really wanted to.

She pressed her knuckles into her abdomen. If only she could have had every organ removed after the last miscarriage, instead of just getting her uterus scraped. Maybe then she'd feel nothing except emptiness.

"For God's sake," she sneered after catching sight of herself in the cloudy mirror near the front door. "What a load of melodrama."

Her mother had been a fine melodramatist, according to her dad. Meg remembered her as being sweet, fanciful and loving. But also weak. Emotional. Needy.

"Not fit for ranch life" had been the common diagnosis after Richard Lennox's wife, Jolene, had slid from the occasional bleak mood into a deep depression. The townspeople had clucked over the way their daughter had been allowed to run wild.

They hadn't known the worst of it. Not until, at age eleven, Meg had found her mother cold and lifeless in her bed, bottles of pills scattered across the blankets. In the community, there'd been whispers of suicide. Her father had refused to accept the possibility. The autopsy had come back as an unintentional overdose.

Meg didn't remember much from that time, except that she'd made up her mind never to be weak like her mother. She'd been too young to realize how difficult her mother's life had been.

Lately, she'd begun to understand.

Meg went into the kitchen, took a look at the clock, then inside the refrigerator. Nothing seemed appetizing. Still, she had to eat. Keep up her strength.

She rubbed at one of her wrist tattoos. Weakness was insidious. It had grown inside her mother until she'd rarely left the bedroom. During Meg's own bad times, she'd battled against the same urge to retreat. And given in far too often.

Not this time. She had nowhere left to run.

She took out the platter of leftover roast beef, added an overripe tomato, a stick of butter. The last of the lettuce had gone to brown slime. A plain sandwich would do, if the bread wasn't moldy.

Room and board. Good Lord. She'd have to cook halfway-decent meals for Rio. Sit with him, eat with him, converse with him.

Incredible.

She reached beneath her sweatshirt, laid her hand against her flat stomach. Her hip bones were prominent. The waistband of her jeans gapped.

Rio, she thought again. Still stunned. *Rio.*

She shouldn't have agreed to give him the job, no matter how much she owed him.

Too uneasy to sit, she carried the sandwich around the house, nibbling at it as she went from space to space. The little-used dining room. The study she avoided whenever possible. The front room, with a river-rock fireplace, her father's dumpy chair and a carpet worn to the nub.

The entry hall was ill lit and gloomy. On her mother's good days, she'd kept it swept and tidy. She'd send Meg out to pick wildflowers for the pitcher on the side table. Now the space was strictly utilitarian. There remained a heap of her father's boots, a tangle of his outdoor clothing. Fishing rods and garden tools leaned haphazardly against the wall. Clods of dried mud had collected where she'd kicked off her own dirty boots.

The sight was dismaying. She'd have to do better. Tomorrow, she'd clean it all away. She'd open the doors and windows.

Meg took a voracious bite of her sandwich. Everything would be better.

The thought came unbidden: *now that Rio's home.*

THE NEXT MORNING, at a window booth in Edna's Eatery, long Treetop's busiest diner, Virginia Carefoot made an unusual fuss over her son. Rio was self-conscious about the curious glances thrown their way, but he put up with the motherly concern. Virginia claimed she had ten years of separation to make up for.

She'd already coaxed him into ordering fruit and granola on the side of his Belgian waffle. She'd stolen a sausage off his plate, since the nitrates weren't good for him. Now that they'd finished their meal and ordered refills on the coffee, she'd moved on to his appearance.

"I can't get used to you with short hair," Virginia said with her head cocked to one side. Her gaze was intense, as if she was memorizing his features. He supposed, like her, he looked older. "You'll let it grow, won't you?"

"I've had short hair for ten years, Ma."

"But now you're home. The army has no more say." For someone who had kowtowed to a boss for as long as Rio could remember, Virginia was a proud woman with definite opinions. Although she tended to be as cautious with words as she was with actions. "You're yourself again."

"Maybe *I* want short hair."

She shook her head. Most Crow men wore their hair long.

Rio couldn't resist teasing her. "I thought I was myself. Making my own decisions."

"Of course." With a decisive click, she set her cup on the saucer. "But you're also my son, and one of the Carefoots."

Because it was easiest, Rio agreed. As a full Crow, she'd never really got his sense of estrangement. To her, he was a Crow first and a Carefoot second, and that was what was important. Having an Anglo father was merely a detail, best forgotten. Try as he had, Rio couldn't compartmentalize his life the way Virginia did with her own. For as long as he'd known what was what, Rio's parentage had remained an unspoken rift between them.

"When are you going to retire?" he asked abruptly.

Virginia drew back. "Why should I retire?"

"You've been working for the Stones for thirty years. Isn't that enough?" He didn't know how she'd lasted so long.

"Still, I'm only fifty-six." She remained a good-looking woman, rounded but vigorous and tough from years of physical labor. Her hair was as much gray as black now, typically pulled back in a low ponytail or wrapped in a bandanna or scarf of some sort. There were a few more lines in her face than he remembered, but Rio didn't really see them unless he looked. She was his mother—the rock-steady cornerstone that had kept him straight, growing up.

He'd shaken her only once, when he'd been arrested for arson that terrible night. Ten years later, after he'd been honorably discharged and had come home for good, she'd hugged him fiercely at the airport, and told him she was finally at peace.

He hadn't had the heart to tell her that his days of lobbing grenades weren't over yet.

"Is it money?" he asked. "Soon, if this book deal works out for me, you'll finally be able to retire. I'll help you out with expenses."

He had to make the offer, even though he knew that money wasn't what kept her at the Stone ranch. Every month of his time in the service, he'd sent her a portion of his paycheck, hoping she would use the extra cushion to gain her independence. But she hadn't wanted that for herself. He had.

Virginia set her mouth so that deep lines carved brackets at either side. "I live very well, thank you. I have what I need."

"You don't have a home of your own."

"No, but I'm at home."

He scoffed. "The ranch."

Her resolve didn't waver. "I've loved it there, Rio."

"Ma, there's no guarantee—"

"Hush." She gave him a warning glance.

Edna's was half filled with breakfast lingerers. Rio, being new back in town, had already drawn a good amount of interest and conversation, including, to his chagrin, an impromptu "Support our troops" rally from four ancient members of the Treetop VFW who held down a corner table every a.m. Better that, he supposed, than a rehashing of the old scandal that had converted him from local success story to just another kid who hadn't managed to rise above his so-called station in life.

Yet.

"I have all the guarantee I need," his mother said stolidly.

"You have—" *Nothing,* he wanted to say, but that

would upset her. Virginia truly believed that her place on the Stone ranch was secure.

"You have me," he amended. "I'm your guarantee."

"Yes, and I'm grateful for that. Having you home is all that's important. If only…" Virginia paused, and Rio saw that she was considering how much to say. She was the practical type. She didn't fight losing battles. Even when he'd signed up for the army, forgoing the college education she'd put such faith in, her disapproval had been muted by resignation.

"I just wish that you hadn't agreed to work for *that* woman." His mother looked down at her capable brown hands, unadorned except for a plain gold band she wore on the ring finger of her right hand. Her "wedding" ring, he'd always assumed. "Are you sure that's necessary?"

"I need a place to stay and an undemanding job."

"There's the money market account." She'd taken every cent he'd given her and invested it. She called the account her grandchildren's college fund.

"No, I'm not touching that." He had his own savings. He'd already dipped into the money to buy a state-of-the-art laptop computer. Although he could have also covered the cost of a room and meals for the next several months, he hadn't been able to resist Meg's ad. Two birds with one stone, so to speak.

His mother tried again. "You could stay at the…"

The invitation died on her lips, withered by Rio's hard stare. He'd sworn he'd never step foot on the Stone ranch again. Not without an invitation. Definitely not as the bastard son of the boss's housekeeper.

Virginia gave in with a grim nod, though she wasn't happy about it. "All right. But keep your distance from her, if you can."

"I intend to," he said forcefully, much too aware of the old saying about the road to hell. "Remember, I have work to do." Work that would keep him apart from Meg even if his intentions didn't.

"Writing. I can hardly comprehend that, either. It doesn't seem like a real job to me."

"You've read the blog?" A couple of years ago, he'd begun writing entries for a soldiers' group blog that had gained a large readership and quite a bit of notoriety. He'd sent his mother the Web site link from Afghanistan but she'd never really commented.

Virginia made a face. "It was too graphic for me."

He smiled an apology. Much of the language had been rough, blunt. Soldiers weren't polite. "I warned you to read only my stuff."

"Yours was hard to take, too. In a different way."

He waited, but that was all she'd say. Typical.

"It may get worse, you know, if I'm published."

"Rio." The way she said his name was like a scolding. "Please reconsider."

"Why? You said it yourself. I'm on my own again. Free and independent. I've accepted my birthright— or lack of one. Do you want me to be ashamed of who I am?"

This was the closest he'd ever come to stating the bald truth to her face. He twisted in the leatherette booth, bringing his fist down on the table with more force than he'd meant to. The crockery rattled. He quickly quieted it. "For chrissake, Ma, this is a new century. There's no real stigma to—"

"That's enough." Color flamed his mother's face. "Can't you write this thing without naming names? Anonymous."

"This *thing?*" He hadn't expected her to understand his compelling need to write his story, to leach the poison out, but he'd hoped that she'd be proud of the accomplishment, at least.

"The book," she said heavily.

"It's a memoir."

Her gaze slid away. "Authors use pen names. It's not unusual."

He forced a negligent shrug. The blog had been written under nicknames—pseudonyms, of a sort— to protect the careers of the soldiers. It wasn't required that he use his own name. His agent, however, had told him that being open to the publicity would be highly beneficial. As well, verification would be required.

Verification of the truth. A truth that would devastate several people who deserved it, but also his mother. Maybe even Meg, for all that she'd put on a good front of not caring what others thought of her.

"I'm thinking about it," he conceded. "Or who

knows? The memoir may not pan out." He wasn't even sure he could write a book in the first place.

"What about fiction?"

"I don't think so." There'd already been enough fiction in his life. His mother had accepted it, even perpetuated it. He wasn't as willing.

"What does *she* say?"

"Meg and I haven't discussed it. She doesn't know that I'm writing a book."

"That won't last, not in Treetop."

"We'll see. The ranch is isolated. She doesn't seem to have much to do with the townspeople."

"Like her father."

Rio had never thought of Meg as antisocial. But she wasn't an ordinary girl, either. She was hard to know, difficult to get along with. Except when it came to the two of them, relating one-on-one. Their friendship had deep roots. The love was more complicated, especially after she'd rejected him the last time.

The *real* last time, he'd decided then, as she skipped town with another guy. That resolution had been easier to keep with thousands of miles between them.

Now, she was already working her way under his skin, into his blood. The old desires were tugging at him.

But, no, he wouldn't take her back. Not again. Even in the unlikely event that she offered. If nothing else, the memoir would prevent that.

"I don't trust her," Virginia went on. "She'll get you into trouble. Again."

"I'm responsible for my own actions, Ma."

Virginia gave an inelegant snort. "Responsible for hers, too."

"Her name is Meg. You used to like her, or at least you tried to befriend her."

"She was young then. A skinny child with no mother, growing up practically wild. I felt sorry for her."

"That didn't change just because she got older." Older, but also tougher, wilder, even more daring. Sometimes, she'd scared even Rio.

Primarily, she'd confused him. He'd been dealing with his own adolescent turmoil. He hadn't been equipped to handle the strange new way that Meg made him feel, with her ripening body and her growing awareness of how boys, even men, reacted to her.

Virginia was still fretting. "She'll be a distraction for you."

Rio looked out the window. Sure enough. A charge went through him at the mere sight of Meg.

"There she is now."

His mother's eyes narrowed. "Speak of the devil."

Meg was across the street in the Food King parking lot. She loaded grocery bags into her trunk, her jacket hanging open and a long red scarf tied loosely around her neck. The wind caught at her hair, making his heart leap. Memories.

Good intentions…

"I'm going to help her." He stood and pulled out his

wallet. "Why don't you come over and say hi. Meg asked after you."

Virginia's mouth was drawn. "I'll finish my coffee."

"Give me five minutes." He loped across Range Street, the two-lane road that was Treetop's main thoroughfare. The cold was biting. "Meg! Hold up."

"Hey, Rio," she said with a natural ease that was a big improvement over the previous day's tension. She brushed her hair aside. "Morning."

He pulled up, grabbed one of the remaining bags and set it in the back of her car. "Planning to feed an army?"

"Nope. Only you." Her smile was a sun flickering behind clouds. "I remember how you used to eat. Like a voracious army, leaving no flapjack unturned."

He looked into the next bag. A giant sack of green beans and a frozen apple pie. "Mmm, lunch. You'll be sorry you hired me."

She became brisk, shoving the last bag at him and rolling away the cart. "I'm already sorry, but not for that."

"What? Why?"

"It's—" She squinted. "Just second thoughts. Is that your mother?"

Virginia clearly sat in the diner window, her face a pale oval behind the dark glass. Looming large across the building's low eaves the retro sign in tall turquoise letters spelled out EDNA'S. "We were having breakfast."

Meg waved. After a moment, Virginia lifted her hand.

"You know what's funny? I haven't run into your mother since I've been back." Meg slanted a look at him. "But I suppose I haven't been off the ranch a whole lot."

"Neither has she. You're both homebodies." He gritted his teeth. His mother's idea of home didn't match his own. And yet he couldn't argue that she wasn't content.

"That's a new one for me." Meg shut the trunk. "Speaking of home, I'm heading back there after a quick stop at the feed store. When will you be along? Do you need more time?"

He watched her fiddle with the zipper on her jacket.

"When do you want me?" The question felt loaded.

She knew it, too, answering him only with a wry expression.

"I can pack and check out in five minutes," he said.

"You're not staying at the Stones'?"

"No."

She didn't ask why, but a worry line appeared between her eyebrows. "I did some work on the cabin last night, but it's still a mess."

"That's okay. I can help fix it up."

This time, her smile stayed a while longer. Someday he'd get her to laugh again. "You're sure in a rush to start shoveling shit."

"Is that my job? Damn. You never said I'm your new Rooney. Next you'll be peppering my snuff."

"R-r-right. When you start walking bowlegged, I'll let you know." She tossed her hair over her shoulder and got in the car. It was a red Camaro with Nevada plates, a dozen dings and rust spots past the point of well maintained. "Listen. There's no rush. Come by any time next week, if you'd rather."

So she *wasn't* ready. "I want to get settled in."

"What about your mother? Wouldn't you like to spend more time with her?"

"She's not going anywhere." And neither was he. It was time to face the past. Maybe he couldn't fix the things that had gone wrong or enact some kind of ideal reunion with his father, but he could learn how to live with the truth—openly. Writing the memoir could turn out to be a healing experience, not just a divisive one.

Meg said, in a rather stilted way, "Tell Virginia that she's welcome at Wild River anytime, if she wants to visit with you."

Rio nodded. Meg put up her window, withdrawing into the dark interior as she reached for the ignition. She must have known, or sensed, that his mother still blamed her for the supposed ruination of Rio's future. He gave her credit for making the first overture, however small.

"I will," he said, though she was driving away. He waved at the departing car.

From Edna's, Virginia watched, her face placid but her worry palpable. Rio told himself he knew what he was doing.

CHAPTER THREE

THE NEXT MORNING, Meg woke to the smell of frying bacon. She burrowed deeper into her bed, awash with memories of a time when her mother was alive and active. They had filled out the small kitchen table perfectly—two parents, a little girl who swung her legs against the chair rungs, and Rooney, a grizzled, guffawing "uncle" who used to give her quarters for candy and gum.

Mornings for the past few months had been ascetic. Caffeine was her only remaining vice. Sitting at the same table with the coffeemaker at hand, she'd made lists of chores, lists for the feed store and hardware store, lists of low-cost ways to advertise her training stable. She'd never been a list maker before, but she'd thought that having it all written down would get her going, and doing.

Some days, it worked. Others, not.

She'd learned soon enough that there wasn't a list on earth that could write away her loneliness.

This morning was different. Rio was in the house. She was up and out of bed, showered and half-dressed before she realized it.

When she entered the kitchen, he was laying strips of bacon on a folded paper towel. Tall, brown, in a red plaid flannel shirt, jeans and stocking feet. A lock of black hair fell in his eyes. He looked up and flashed a white smile. "Morning, Meg. I started breakfast."

"That's not your job. But thanks." Her stomach growled. "I guess I'm starved."

"Good. You're too thin."

"Yeah, well, you look like you could use a few home-cooked meals yourself."

"That's what my mother says."

Rio's mother. He'd brought her up several times yesterday, as they were working on the cabin. He'd kept it all casual, but Meg had the feeling that he was planning to get them together and talking, despite their agreement that he was here for a job, not a lovey-dovey reunion.

She did have some fond memories of Virginia Carefoot. For a time, the woman had seemed like just about an ideal, motherly kind of mother to Meg, even when her own had still been alive. But then she'd grown up and Virginia had become quietly disapproving of the relationship between her upstanding son and the town's bad girl. From a more mature perspective, Meg could hardly blame Mrs. Carefoot for that. She'd been dead right in predicting that Meg would lead Rio to a sad end.

"You go feed the horses," she told him. "I'll finish breakfast."

"I already fed them."

"Oh." She glanced at the clock. "I overslept." She would have sworn that having Rio on the ranch would keep her tossing and turning, but instead she'd conked out for a solid nine hours—the longest she'd slept in years. "I'll start setting an alarm."

"No problem. I can take over the morning feeding. I'm closer to the barn, in the bunkhouse. The horses wake me anyway."

"Um, okay, then how about pancakes?" She reached for the canister of flour. A carton of eggs was open on the counter. She cracked several into a bowl, glad to have something to do with her hands. He was watching and that made her skittish.

"Sure, if they're apple."

"Why not." Yesterday, she'd bought more produce than she had in the previous ninety days. A mixing bowl filled with Macintoshes sat on the table. "If you slice them up, nice and thin."

He got a knife and sat at the table. She drained the grease from the cast-iron frying pan, the same one that had always been used at the ranch. She added milk and baking soda to the mixing bowl and began whisking the batter. "So…you seem to have settled in all right."

Her scalp prickled from the sensation of Rio's gaze on the back of her head. "I'm at home here," he said easily. "Nothing's changed."

"Except you're sleeping in the bunkhouse."

"We did that a few times. Remember?"

Hell, yes, she remembered. As kids, they'd thought it was great fun to take over the cabin on the rare nights that Rooney was gone. They'd played at being cowboys, with a campfire and beans heated in the can and served on tin plates. They'd rolled out their sleeping bags and told ghost stories and dirty jokes that they hadn't half understood, until finally they couldn't keep their eyes open any longer.

But there'd been other nights, too, when they'd grown older. In the cabin, in the barn, even, once or twice, in Meg's bedroom. Her father would have banned Rio from the ranch if he'd ever caught them. That had been half the thrill for her.

"I remember." She poured a dollop of the batter into the pan and watched the sizzling edges as if they were mesmerizing. *Remember* was a dangerous word for them.

Rio nudged her. "The apples."

She stepped away. "Go ahead."

He laid slices in the frying pancake. "Remember when we tried to roast apples over the campfire?"

"Sure." That word again—*remember.* Was he deliberately making her recall how easy things used to be between them? "We stuck them on sharpened sticks. They came out all black and crisp outside and raw inside."

"Those were good times."

"Yeah." Meg retreated. Leaving Rio to flip the pancakes, she snatched one of her lists off the sloppy pile of notepads, instruction manuals and several outdated phone books on top of the fridge. "We should go over the day's chores. Get it straight how things are going to be around here."

"Fuel first," he insisted. "I need a hot cup of coffee and a bellyful of apple pancakes before I can face my first day as your stable boy."

"You started yesterday."

They had emptied the cabin, scrubbed the floor and sink, scraped and painted trim, washed the window. Her final task had been to hang a pair of curtains she'd fashioned out of two linen dish towels printed with strawberries and watermelon slices. Rio had laughed and said that Rooney would have never stood for such a womanly touch, but fortunately *he* was secure in his masculinity.

That was when Meg had scrammed. After soaking in a hot bath and thinking a little too long about Rio's very secure masculinity, she'd decided she'd have to reiterate their position as boss and employee. She would assign him duties that ensured there'd be as little contact as possible between them during an average day. They'd already become too chummy.

She ducked her head over the list as he put a platter of pancakes between them. Sharing a meal in the cozy kitchen wasn't helping her cause.

"Today," she announced, "you can work on repairing the fences." That would keep him out of her way.

"Shouldn't I muck out the stalls first?"

"But I was going to groom the horses."

"Exactly. They'll be out of their stalls."

"Of course." She forked two pancakes onto her plate and four onto his.

He buttered them and added syrup, looking too content for her peace of mind. "I don't bite, Meg. Hell, I won't even talk to you if you don't want me to."

She frowned. He'd had a knack for knowing what she was thinking and feeling. Except the one time that she'd held a huge secret so deep inside that not even Rio had suspected. He had known that *something* was wrong, but she'd led him to believe that she was just nervous about their upcoming high school graduation and her plan to leave home immediately afterward.

"It's not that." Her eyes darted to his face. He was studiously slicing through his stack and didn't look up. "We can be friendly, sort of. We just can't be close. Not the way we used to be."

He reached for the coffee, still too relaxed. "Why?"

She became very interested in chewing. He was stirring milk into his coffee, the spoon going around and around until she knew that he wasn't as indifferent as he portrayed.

She hooked her feet on the chair rung. "Too much happened. And too much time has gone by."

"But if we got it all into the open, wouldn't that be better?"

"Not for me."

Rio's expression didn't change, but she could tell he was disappointed in her. *Join the club,* she thought. *I may not be much good for closure, but I'm an expert at cutting my losses and moving on.*

He jerked the spoon from the mug. "Whatever you say, boss."

RICHARD LENNOX HAD RUN a good-size herd of cattle back in the day, when the market had thrived and there'd been more than one cowboy in the bunkhouse. Lean years had cut the herd in half by the time Meg had been allowed to work the cattle alongside the men. After she'd gone and Rooney had passed away, the word around town had been that Lennox was a broken man. He'd reduced the herd even more and scraped by on his own. Sometime along the way, a large parcel of the ranch land had been sold.

What acreage remained was remote but prime, reaching as far as the mountains to the south and culminating in a small, deep canyon to the west. Meg could have made a nice sum by selling it, but she was her father's daughter, likely to turn her nose up at the large ranch corporations or California tourists who'd be the buyers.

While much of the land was free range, the pastures closest to the house were strung with barbed wire. That meant a lot of fence to ride.

Rio could think of worse jobs. Plenty of them. Only months ago, he'd been stuck in a mountaintop outpost in Kunar Province, barely surviving the grinding heat and dust and stones while dreaming of the cold, clear Wyoming skies. Ten years away hadn't made him forget what it was like to breathe air so pure you felt glad to be alive.

This morning, the wind sweeping off the mountains had a bite. He pulled up the collar of his jacket before returning a steadying hand to the reins. Meg had put him aboard her horse Renny, short for Renegade. The bay gelding had some age on him, but he'd capered like a two-year-old as they rode toward the foothills.

Clouds like thick cotton wadding moved slowly across the sky, hiding the sun. Rio remembered long hours spent down in a bunker while insurgents fired on the camp, the sun beaming relentlessly down on him and his infantry unit. In those hours, he'd often think of Meg. Happy and productive, he'd hoped, but maybe as lonely without him as he was without her.

The war had dragged on. He'd seen soldiers killed. More wounded. Many lost arms or legs. Eventually he'd come to understand that Meg was *his* phantom limb. A pain so real it woke him up at night.

At his discharge from the army, he'd overcome the temptation to search for her. He hadn't considered that he'd find her right here, in Treetop, even though that made sense. They'd both returned like homing pigeons.

He studied the landscape that had once been so familiar, recognizing certain trees, particular rocks.

It seemed unbelievable that they were living on the ranch together. Except that the Meg he'd been remembering all this time was not the person she was now.

Would she become familiar again, too?

He wanted to relearn her, but she wasn't ready to give him any specifics about what and where she'd been for the past decade, beyond a list of short-term jobs she'd held down. He couldn't blame her. He didn't want to talk either, which was why he'd taken to writing as an outlet.

Still, this was only their second day together. They had time. And nothing to keep them apart, except fences of their own making. Which, Rio well knew, were the most insurmountable of all.

SEVERAL HOURS LATER, he gripped a pair of pliers with a hand rubbed raw. Rookie move, forgetting his gloves. Wearing the proper gear was basic cowboy knowledge, but he hadn't done ranch work in a long time.

He put some muscle into his task and stretched the broken wire taut, then attached it with an efficient twist to one of the extra lengths he'd brought along. That'd hold. Especially since he didn't figure Meg would be running stock up here in the high pasture anytime soon.

He doffed his cap, an army-issue camo job, and wiped his forehead with his sleeve. It was past noon. The sun had risen above the clouds and was warm enough to heat the back of his neck. Renny nosed the dry grass, looking for green, tugging the reins as he stretched his neck toward a tempting mouthful.

The last thing he needed was to lose his horse, so many miles from the house. It'd be a long walk back. Meg would tease him mercilessly, probably bring up the last time his horse had arrived at Wild River an hour before him.

Might be worth it, he mused, to get her to re-member—or rather, acknowledge—their history. She remembered; he knew she did. That was why she was being so standoffish.

Freeing the reins from the fence post, he led Renny along the fence line, coming to a section that was beyond spot repair. Rusty barbed wire lay in snarls in the buffalo grass, tangled in the branches of a fallen tree.

Sloop and Meg appeared on the rise, loping through the golden grass. The horse's pale mane and tail made a bright flag in the sunshine. Meg sat astride, slim and quiet in the saddle. Rio's gut tightened, the way it did when he watched a hawk soar above the mountains, or the sunset burn a line across the desert. She'd always been his own personal force of nature.

She pulled up alongside Renny. "Problems?"

He gestured at the downed fence. "I'll have to move the tree, then run new strands."

Meg flicked the reins against her mount's neck to keep him from nipping at Renny. "All right."

"Barbed wire is no good for horses."

"Well, no. But I can't afford board fences right now."

"Maybe not up here, but how much grazing land do you need, with only three horses in the barn?"

"There will be more. Until then, I suppose the home pasture will do."

"Then why'm I out here?" Rio caught the sheepish cast to her expression before she glanced away. "You were just trying to keep me busy," he accused her.

She turned Sloop in a tight circle. "No…"

"You wanted me out of the way."

"That's not it," she protested. With small conviction.

"My time would have been better spent in the barn. The feed room's neglected. There's enough space between some of the boards to see daylight." He stowed the pliers and wire cutters in the saddlebag. "I won't be much use to you if you can't stand to have me around."

"You're wrong." She'd never admit defeat. "It was just that the good weather won't hold for long. I thought the fences should be taken care of first."

"Busywork," he groused, giving the weather-worn fence post a shove. It rocked. "You need new posts, too."

"Next time I'm in town, I'll price lumber. Maybe we can do the home pasture for now." She looked relieved that he'd let her off the hook. "Anyway, I rode out to see if you were hungry for lunch."

"That wasn't necessary. I packed a sandwich and a thermos of coffee."

Her eyebrows went up. "When did you manage that?"

"After breakfast. You were lurking on the back porch, trying to avoid me."

"I was pacing, not lurking. I had a craving for a cigarette." She wheeled Sloop around. "Leave this section for now. Just fix what you can."

"Waste of time," he called, forestalling her departure.

She glanced back. "What?"

"There's no need to send me off to Outer Mongolia, Meg. I was planning to keep to myself anyway. When you want to be rid of me, all you have to do is say the word."

She didn't seem to know how to respond.

He lifted the second flap of the saddlebag and took out the thermos. "You could even safely share my coffee and sandwich, with no danger of camaraderie." *Let alone intimacy.*

"I rode out here to be sure you got your lunch, didn't I?"

"But I'll bet you had no intention of eating any yourself. At least not with me." He shook his head. "You've got to learn how to relax around me."

Her lashes lowered. "I don't seem to know how to treat you anymore. What do you suggest?"

"First off, don't treat me at all. You're thinking too much when you should be natural. Second, climb down off that horse and have a sip of coffee."

"I'm weaning myself off caffeine," she said, but she dismounted.

He tied Renny to the rickety post and strolled to an outcropping of rock and sagebrush. "You had coffee this morning."

"I allow myself one cup with breakfast." She smoothed

her horse's reins between her hands. "I gave up all my other vices—alcohol, cigarettes, swearing."

Men, he silently added, though he didn't know that for sure. He was guessing, by her antsiness around him, that she hadn't been with a man for some time.

"How come?" he asked.

She shrugged. "Just had enough of them, is all."

"I hope you weren't sick." She had the gaunt look of someone who'd been through the wringer, one way or another. He supposed he had the same look.

"Not exactly what you'd call—" She pressed her lips together. "You see? This is what I wanted to avoid. All this talk. The questions."

"Uh-huh. And what sort of conversation would you prefer, ma'am? The common weather variety, I suppose." He pointed to the sky. "Chilly and clear. Partly sunny, with intermittent clouds. It's turned into a fine autumn day."

She nudged at a mossy stone with the toe of her boot. "Go tell it to the Weather Channel."

He screwed the top back on the thermos. The coffee had warmed him from the inside, the sun from the outside. Yet he was still cold. "It's going to be a long winter, Meg."

"It always is."

"But with just you and me here, especially if you keep on acting so prickly…"

Sloop pulled on the reins, snatching at the grass. Absently Meg tugged back. Her eyes were narrowed on Rio's. "What are you saying?"

"Ease up. Pull in the quills. I'm not an enemy."

She shortened the reins, bringing the horse's head up. Her face was unnaturally pale beneath the two spots of ruddy color in her cheeks.

"You know it," he added. *She had to.* "You know me."

"It's been ten years."

"Not that much has changed, no matter how long it's been." He wanted to shorten the distance between them, but it wasn't going to be that easy. "You can trust me, Meg."

She threw the reins around Sloop's neck and reached for the stirrup. He admired her athletic grace as she swung her leg over the saddle. And, admittedly, her fine shape. Even skinny, she filled out her jeans very well.

"If you're staying all winter," she added. "I guess I'll find out."

He watched her ride away, loping again, faster than she should have, not looking back. He was satisfied with himself for making even a small amount of progress with her, until a disarming thought struck him.

Given what a large part of his life Meg had once been, there was the enormous likelihood that he'd be writing about her in a very intimate way. She wouldn't like that. In fact, she'd hate it.

Yet he'd just said that she could trust him.

If the book deal went through, it would prove him to be a liar.

CHAPTER FOUR

MEG AND RIO SETTLED into a routine over the next several days, although she could never be entirely at ease with him. There were too many uncomfortable moments when their idle chitchat turned serious or old shared memories arose from some innocent remark. It seemed to her that their history lurked in the shadows, ready to spring up as suddenly and as lethal as a rattler.

Then there were the instances when Rio got too close physically. Meg was accustomed to avoiding the past. But practically living with a man, especially one as vital as Rio, was disturbing in an immediate way that was impossible to ignore.

She handled that by taking a big step back. Literally and figuratively, no matter how strong the temptation to succumb grew. Since the chemistry between them would always be there, she was counting on getting better with practice. Better at avoiding him. Stronger at resisting.

Not that Rio pushed. Or even tried. He hadn't made a single move. He was, in fact, scrupulous about giving her the space she needed. Which was fine with her.

Until she began noticing that he seemed to want to keep away from her as much as she tried to avoid him.

That made her wonder.

Sure, he had reason. Not only had she left him, she'd been responsible for almost sending him to jail. But, amazingly, he didn't seem bitter or angry. He'd practically ordered her to get more comfortable with him.

How could she when he never stuck around?

Every evening, for instance, he retreated to the bunkhouse right after supper. She was grateful at first. Then restless. And curious. There was nothing to entertain him in the cabin—not even a TV or radio. She'd offered to have the satellite-dish company come out to install a second receiver, but Rio had refused. He'd claimed he didn't watch a lot of TV.

After a week, she'd mentioned that he could hang around after dinner if he liked. It wasn't that she was looking for company, she'd justified to herself. The baseball playoffs would soon be starting and she'd felt obliged to offer since the Mariners were contenders and he'd once been a fan.

Again, Rio had said no. Then no to a movie on DVD, too. Even when she'd gone out of her way to choose one of the action flicks he'd once preferred.

After that, she was determined not to offer again.

Yet she couldn't stop wondering what he did with himself. He didn't drive into town, not even on Sunday, his day off. He'd barely put in an appearance at all that day, except when he'd asked to borrow Renny. He'd gone off on a horseback ride to Eagle Rock, a craggy point near the canyon they'd discovered as kids, pretending they were Lewis and Clark on expedition. He hadn't asked her to go along, though of course she'd have declined if he had.

So, yeah. She was getting exactly what she'd thought she wanted.

"Great," she said, standing at the stove scrambling eggs on the seventh day of October. The date was circled on the insurance company calendar she'd hung beneath her mother's old cuckoo clock. "Just great. Yep. I am greatly relieved."

At least she *should* be.

Rio let himself in the back door. "Talking to yourself is a sign of senility or loneliness, I don't remember which." He scraped his boots on the welcome mat. "What you need is a dog."

"What you need is a hat," she said, glancing at the reddened tips of his ears. "Aren't you cold?"

He rubbed his hands together before crossing to the coffeemaker and pouring a cup. "I'll get a hat if you'll get a dog. Every ranch needs a dog."

She thrust a plate of eggs and buttered English muffins at him. "A dog requires care and feeding. A hat is just a hat."

"Except when it's a cowboy hat. Should I get white or black?"

"Gray."

"Spotted or solid?"

"Huh?" She pictured him in black-and-white cowhide. No way.

"Long hair or short?"

Her eyes went to Rio's hair. The military cut was growing like stinkweed. The ends of his hair were already long enough to brush his collar. He looked more like the boy she remembered. Or maybe it was that she'd been getting used to the man he'd become, stranger though he'd remained.

"The dog," he said.

"Right." She forked up her eggs. Her appetite had improved. In the short time since Rio had moved to the ranch, she'd put on a pound or two. She figured that was just a by-product of feeling obligated to feed him well. Not anything to do with being happier. "I like mutts."

"What size? You haven't turned into the kind of girl who goes for an itty-bitty pocket dog, have you?"

She rolled her eyes. "You have to ask?"

His gaze lingered on the layered long-sleeved tees and favorite pair of Levi's 501s that had practically become her uniform. "Guess not."

She pushed away her plate with more force than necessary. "Today's the auction."

"I remembered." She saw that he had. He was handsome in a fresh white shirt and practically new jeans. She did *not* let her gaze linger.

He indicated her almost-full plate. "Nerves took your appetite?"

"I don't have anything to be nervous about."

"No? Then I guess it's only me."

She frowned. Rio had always been the solid, silent type, but she didn't remember him being so maddeningly obtuse. All week, he'd kept to himself, giving away nothing of his thoughts or plans.

How dare he follow her separation edict so strictly! If she hadn't been so frustrated, she would have laughed at the irony.

Instead, she frowned more deeply, "What are you talking about?"

"You and me," he said easily enough. "We'll be out in public together for the first time since you hired me. Kind of a debut, you know?" Cocking his head to one side, he said, "We'll be the center of attention."

"Heaven forbid," she said, but she wasn't convinced. "You're wrong. No one will care."

Fortunately, the auction was in Laramie, over a hundred and fifty miles away. "As far as anyone's concerned, we're simply boss and employee, minding our own business." They might run into acquaintances, but it wouldn't be like parading down Range Street hand in hand, with everyone from her neighbors, the Vaughns, to the gang at Edna's gawking at them.

Rio tossed off a cocky salute, a habit he'd taken to whenever she got to sounding too bossy. "Whatever you say, Sarge."

She wrinkled her nose. "If you're finished with breakfast, let's go." She cleared the table, scraping the dishes and leaving them in the sink instead of loading the dishwasher. "The riding horses won't be on the block until the afternoon, but I want to get there early enough to inspect the available stock."

"What are you looking for?"

"Young, green and cheap." She wiped her hands on her back pockets. "Will you help? You always had an eye for horseflesh."

His gaze had skimmed across her. Whatever he'd seen had made his eyes gleam like jet. "Sure, I'll help."

After the week together but apart, Meg felt good to have him look at her with some interest again. She stepped away quickly, before the urge to prolong the moment took hold. "Let's get a move on. It's at least a two-hour drive."

THEY TOOK HER CAR. Meg kept the radio on for most of the drive, punching the buttons to switch stations whenever she became impatient. Rio teased her for the short attention span. She teased him right back for stabbing his left foot on the floor every time she zipped around a slow vehicle.

"You drive the same way you used to." The car swerved. He made an exaggerated grab for the door handle. "I felt less at risk during a mortar attack."

"Balderdash. I haven't been in an accident in two years."

"Two whole years, huh. That's comforting, but…" He chuckled. "'Balderdash'?"

"An experiment." She lifted her chin. "Remember,

I'm trying to cut down on the curse words. But there aren't many options that don't sound as corny as Nebraska. Horsefeathers, baloney, bull puckey." She waved a hand at an approaching vehicle wavering toward the center line. "Golly gee, look at that jerkweed in the bat-rastard Jeep!" She scoffed. "You see? It's hopeless."

Rio shifted his legs. They were too long for the Camaro. "What's with the self-improvement kick? No drinking, no swearing, no caffeine, no, uh, dates. Is it self-improvement or self-denial?"

"Aren't they the same thing?"

"Not always."

"Name a situation where it's not."

"Easy. I went to night school for eight years, off and on. I improved myself with no pain."

"I don't know about that." She considered. "You gave up all your free time. That's a denial."

"Hmm. Maybe…"

"Damn straight." She bit her bottom lip. "Oops. I meant darn tootin'."

He laughed. "A few damns and hells don't shock me."

"I'm not doing it for you."

His mouth canted. "Prickly."

They rode in silence for a few miles before she cleared her throat. "Did you really do that? Get a college degree?"

"Yes."

"I'm glad."

He looked at her sidelong. There was a world of

meaning in those two words, since she was the reason he'd forfeited his scholarship to college. By his reckoning, the delay had been worth it. Back then, he'd have done anything for her. Possibly he still would.

But did that include deep-sixing—or at least severely altering—his memoir?

"What did you study?" she asked. "I remember when you wanted to be a biologist."

"I was seven. And into frogs."

"After that it was a mechanical engineer."

"Only because I thought that meant I'd design cars."

"And you were going to be a baseball player, too."

"Every kid has that dream." He'd dropped the idea pretty fast when Billy Stone had turned nasty over his father giving Rio a baseball glove for his birthday, an extremely rare gift that neither boy had known how to handle. Billy had been chubby and awkward, without an athletic bone in his body. Being only a few years apart in age, they'd buddied around some as youngsters. As they'd grown older, Billy had become more competitive over his father's limited time and attention.

"What about you?" Rio asked Meg. "I don't remember you having a burning ambition for anything except leaving—"

Her wince stopped him short.

"What did I say?"

"Nothing."

Burning ambition. Stupid choice of words, but apologizing would make it worse.

Although he sincerely doubted that it had been deliberate, the fire she'd set on the night she'd finally run away for good had burned the Vaughns' old hay barn to the ground. Two squad cars and the volunteer fire department had shown up, along with half the town. Rio had turned himself in early that morning, when Deputy Sophie Ryan had come to the Stone ranch saying that he'd been spotted leaving the barn before the fire. No fool, the deputy had pressed Rio hard on the question of Meg's whereabouts. He'd insisted he'd been the only one there.

They'd had no choice but to believe him, especially after he'd taken the deal the judge had offered at what was supposed to be his arraignment. The judge, a Stone family friend, had been pressured to hurry the case along…and keep the senator's name out of it. Rio was given a choice. Join the army or face charges. For Meg's sake, he'd capitulated. Even so, his downfall had been the talk of the town. In fact, given the pace of life in Treetop, the arson was probably still the most notorious crime in recent history.

"You never got to college?" he asked Meg.

"You know how I felt about school." She thrust her head forward, her fingers tense on the wheel. She was speeding fifteen miles above the limit.

He returned to her question. "I went in planning to study business, but I came out with a degree in contemporary literature. My favorite class was creative writing."

"You're kidding."

"Not what you expected from a rank-and-file leatherhead?"

"Well, no. But I always knew you'd accomplish anything you set your mind to." She gave him a pointed glance. "So how come you're my stable hand?"

He shrugged. "Call it a holding pattern."

"Holding for what?"

"I'm working on that."

He didn't want to tell her about the book. Not just because publication would prove him a liar. It was also her cynicism. And that she was holding back her own secrets.

But the main reason was that he'd only just begun to work his way into the project. It was still too private and new. For the past week, he'd been expanding the pieces he'd written as previous blog entries, trying to shape them into some kind of proposal for the publishers. He wasn't convinced he had enough of a story to make a memoir beyond his experiences in Afghanistan, from brutal to banal.

The more personal revelations were a trickier proposition. So far he hadn't touched them. Turning over the rocks and digging up the dirt, especially in public, would take every ounce of dogged grit he possessed. Ruthlessness, too.

With some of those involved, like his biological father, he could be ruthless. Near to it, anyway.

But with Meg? That was harder to imagine. He'd never been capable of hurting her. This time, he would have to.

THEY ARRIVED at the auction, which was held in an immense barn at an exposition center. Leaving the low-slung Camaro among a lot filled with SUVs, trucks pulling trailers, and other gas guzzlers, they made their way inside. After stopping to register, they headed directly to the stalls and a small holding corral where the riding horses were being kept. The air was ripe with the earthy scents of leather, livestock and fodder.

"Pass over the older horses," Meg said, her gaze sweeping the backstage scene. She paused beside a black mare, watching a man in a trucker cap run his hands over the horse's near front leg.

He spat a stream of tobacco juice onto the paved aisle way. "Splints."

"Curable," Meg said, passing by. "But the spavined withers aren't."

Rio nodded. "So you wouldn't say no to a horse with an issue that can be fixed with TLC?"

"That depends. If the deal is good enough, I'll invest the time." She stood looking into a stall with her hands shoved into the pockets of the denim jacket she'd lined with a hoodie. "I'm, uh, not that flush with expendable cash. I need to make smart buys."

He peered into the stall. "Beautiful horse. Young, too."

She shook her head. "Too much breeding and manners. I can't consider this type, even green broke. They're sure to go for a price far out of my range."

They continued the search, stopping to discuss a few of the likelier prospects with the sellers. One rancher had brought in a small group of fractious mustangs that were tightly fastened to the corral fence.

"Straight off the range," the fellow claimed. Both Rio and Meg knew better than that. The Bureau of Land Management did not grant title to wild mustangs until after the first year of adoption. They evaluated the rancher's stock, exchanging skeptical looks over their ragged shape.

One mare, dappled a strawberry roan, was extremely shy, throwing her head up against the short length of her lead rope, swaying her hindquarters in a futile attempt to back away from them. Her tail lashed against the dark foal haltered at her side. They were ungroomed, stuck with mud and burrs.

"Genuine mustangs, both of 'em," the rancher said. "Colt's six months old. Ready to be weaned. I'm splittin' them into two lots."

Meg stepped away without touching the pair. "That mare's practically wild."

"Yep. Never had a saddle on her."

"How'd you come by her?"

"This bunch here wandered onto my land. Me 'n a few boys rounded 'em up."

"I'll bet." Meg scowled.

Rio nodded at her. The rancher must think they were fools willing to fall for a tall tale, since the mare's BLM freeze mark—identifying symbols on the left side of her neck—was clearly evident.

"How old?" he asked, keeping his expression blank.

The rancher spat. "Vet said four, maybe five years, tops."

Six or seven, Rio calculated.

"She'd make a fine lady's riding horse, once you get her cleaned up."

"That's debatable." Meg was remarkably restrained. She shook her head. "Sorry. Not what I'm looking for. Too much work."

The seller addressed Rio. "She'd make a good breeder, too." He cackled. "Might kick the hell outta the stallion first."

"Come on," Meg snapped. She'd already moved on to the next seller. After one glance at the broken-down old workhorse she kept going.

"Did you see the scars on that mustang?" she asked Rio, stopping beside a paint gelding who watched the activity with white-rimmed eyes. A young couple was talking with the seller about the horse's temperament. Meg moved in and stroked the paint's neck until he calmed enough to lower his head and snuffle her palm.

Rio stood beside her. "Sure, I saw the scars. Some were old bite and kick marks. Most wild mustangs have them."

"Yes, but a few were fresh. There were rope burns, too, even around her fetlocks."

"I'm not disagreeing. There's no doubt that mare's been treated rough."

"I wonder how he *really* acquired her. I'd like to save her." Meg sighed. "But I can't. No use asking for trouble I can't afford."

"Don't worry. She'll go to a better home. Someone will take her."

"And probably for more than I can pay, anyway. But you know what happens to some of the older horses."

At auctions like these, there were always buyers representing the slaughterhouses prowling about, looking for the old, the lame, the untamed. Any horse that could be bought dirt cheap.

"What about the colt?" Rio suggested. "You could do something with him."

"It'd be years before he could be sold as a fully trained riding horse. I need to turn a profit before that." She ran her hand along the paint's neck. Though the horse settled beneath her steady touch, he was still watching the crowd with a nervous eye. "What do you think of this one?"

"Flashy horse. High strung. That'll put some of the bidders off, but he'll still go for top dollar."

"Yeah, you're right." Even so, Meg stayed and spoke to the seller, making a few notes on the horse before she and Rio moved on.

Eventually they stopped at a stand selling hot dogs and hamburgers. By the time they'd scarfed down a quick lunch at the counter, the last herds of goats and sheep had been ushered bleating from the ring.

The horse sale was about to begin. Meg and Rio went to find seats in the rows of bleachers.

Someone in the crowd waved. "Hey-ah, Meg! Meg Lennox!" A woman who looked vaguely familiar to Rio had popped up from the stands. She had short brown hair and an extra twenty pounds. "I heard you were back in town. Come on over and sit with us, why dontcha?"

"Queenie. Hi." Meg waved. "Thanks, but I want to get a seat down front."

"Are you bidding?"

"Yes, I hope to."

"Then you must be planning to stick around." The woman glanced at Rio. Her eyes got big. "Oh my goodness. I remember *you*, Rio Carefoot!" Smiling hugely, she set her hands on her hips. "Bet you don't know me. Here's a hint—we went to high school together." She included Meg with a nod. "All three of us."

"'Course I know you," he said. "Queenie Briggs." She'd been less chubby in school but just as outgoing. The kind of girl who organized charity drives, decorated for the prom and led the troops in 4H and Girl Scouts.

Queenie beamed. "You do remember! I've changed since then. Gained two hundred pounds. His name is Chuck Davis and he's down there somewhere, making arrangements for the baby goats we bought. We live in Laramie now, he works at the stockyards and I'm a bank teller, and we've got two kids, a boy and a girl. They're getting ready to start in 4H. Phoebe wanted a pony, but for now we're making do with a couple of goats and a hutchful of rabbits."

Queenie stopped talking long enough to glance significantly from Rio to Meg and back to him. Her mouth puckered and her cheeks inflated like a balloon about to burst. "Woo! Look at you two. Together again. Just like the old days."

"Not really," Meg said quickly. She moved into the aisle and was buffeted by burly ranchers coming and going. "We need to get seats."

Rio raised his eyebrows. If she didn't learn to be more neighborly, she'd end up just like her father.

"Don't run off, Meg," he said, even though he wanted to join her. He wasn't as comfortable in the old hometown as he ought to be, either. Probably because he supposed everyone was still speculating on his fall from grace. Had he been guilty or not?

Huh. Maybe writing the memoir was his way of settling that question for good.

"I'm just getting seats," Meg insisted, moving away.

He shrugged. "Then grab one for me. I'll be there in a minute."

Queenie leaned across the bench seat as if it were the back fence between neighbors. "Whatcha bidding on?"

"Meg's looking at horses."

"That's right. I heard she took over her daddy's ranch. Me and Chuck don't get back to Treetop any too

often, but I've still got friends and family there."
Queenie reached across a couple of people and gave
Rio's shoulder a squeeze. "Nobody told me about you
being back. It's good to have you home safe and sound.
I was praying for ya, over there in Iraq."

"Afghanistan." He clasped her hand. "Thanks."

"Your mom must be tickled pink to have you home.
How's she doing anyhow? I haven't seen her in years,
but I still remember those coconut cupcakes she used
to bring to the school bake sales."

Rio was wishing he'd gone with Meg after all. "She's
doing fine. The same as ever."

"How long have you been home?"

"Couple weeks. I'm keeping a low profile."

Queenie winked. "You 'n Meg, huh? Together again!
You didn't waste any time."

"It's not like that."

She just laughed. "It was always like that, even
when she was going with other boys. And some things
don't change."

He held up a hand. "For real. I'm temporarily
helping her out at the ranch. Don't read too much into
it." Not completely denying his interest, he looked for
Meg's tawny head down front. "I'd better go find her.
She's a slave driver."

He must not have sounded too convincing,
because Queenie gazed at him indulgently. "She's a
lucky girl."

He waved her off.

Meg narrowed her eyes as he took the space beside her. "Have a nice chat?"

"Sure."

"She's going to tell everyone we were here together, you know."

"No big deal."

"Maybe not to you."

"Shouldn't be for you, either." He settled in, taking off his jacket and laying it across one knee. "Unless there's something you need to tell me. Maybe you're still carrying a torch and you're worried the Queenies of the world will see it."

"Carrying a torch!" Meg sputtered. "Tha—that's just—"

"Careful." He tilted toward her. "If you protest too much, I'll think I hit on something."

Her jaw clamped shut. Then she couldn't help herself from responding. "I'm just thinking of the talk there'll be. You know how fast rumors spread in Treetop."

"I never knew you to be so prim that you'd care about a few rumors."

Meg made a face. "I'm not prim."

"Coulda fooled me."

When he said no more, she sat back and blew out a breath. "Sorry." Her eyes flashed, but with a wry self-awareness. "But there *will* be talk. One way or another."

He stared straight ahead. "There's something I should probably tell you about, this thing I'm—"

She shushed him. "Here comes the first horse."

An aged brown gelding had been led into the ring. Rio recognized the horse as one they'd passed over.

Bidding was slow. When the sale was knocked down to a man in the second row, Meg felt sick. "Slaughterhouse," she said out of the side of her mouth.

Rio leaned forward. "Are you certain?"

"They buy up every low-dollar horse. But they're not horses to them—they're fodder."

She gnawed the inside of her cheek while the next horse was auctioned, finally raising her paddle when the action remained sluggish. The man in front quickly outbid her.

Rio put his hand on her arm when she would have upped the bid. "You don't want that horse."

"No, but at least I can make *him* spend more."

"You might also end up with a broken-down old horse. Can you afford the upkeep on a pet that big?"

She sighed. "No."

He patted her hand. "You can't save the world."

There was a minor flurry of bidding and the horse was sold to someone other than the slaughterhouse agent. Meg relaxed. "I guess you'd know better than me, soldier."

"About saving the world? I'd like to think my motives were that noble, but mainly I was just doing my job."

"War as a job?" She rubbed her arms. "Being a stable hand isn't so bad by comparison."

"I'd rather think of it as peacekeeping, but I get what you're saying."

"You don't talk much about it, do you?"

He agreed with a grunt.

"Or is it just—" She stopped.

"Just what?"

"That you don't want to talk to me. Not anymore." She flicked up her paddle, earning a frown from the slaughterhouse man at the front. "Not that I blame you," she added grittily.

"I thought it was the other way around," Rio said. "I mean, it's you who's been avoiding me."

She upped the bid again, on another horse she didn't really want.

"Stop it," he said.

The horse went to the slaughterhouse guy. Meg's face twisted. "I don't know *how.* I don't know how to talk to you anymore."

"There's no secret to it. Be the same as you were."

"That's impossible. I've changed, and so have you."

"In some ways. Not the ones that really count."

"I feel like…" She rocked forward, holding the paddle under her chin. One of the day's better prospects, the nervous paint horse, was led into the ring.

Meg watched intently as the bidding began. Rio thought she'd dropped the conversation until she stole a look at him.

Her voice came low and fast. "I keep thinking that even though you act like everything's cool between us, you haven't forgiven me." Her face was pale, except for two spots of color on her cheekbones. "Not that you should. I did take off and leave you to rot in jail, paying for the crime that *I* committed."

CHAPTER FIVE

RIO DIDN'T REPLY at once. Even though the subject had been on both their minds ever since he'd landed at Wild River, he hadn't expected Meg to bring it up in the middle of an auction. She was using the activity to deflect his focus from the conversation they'd been needing to have.

He wished that it was only the two of them, face-to-face, with nothing to hide. The way they'd once been.

Except that those days were long gone.

Meg waited through several rapid bids before raising her paddle. Then only once more, before reaching her top dollar. Her face was pinched. She made an awkward throat-clearing sound. "Shoot. I can't go higher."

"Bide your time. There are others coming up."

She nodded jerkily, a puppet on a string.

"Meg." Rio ran his knuckles along the outside of her thigh. "Sweet Meg. I forgave you a long time ago."

She flinched. "You *forgave* me? How could you? I was never even there to apologize."

He looked down at his hands. He had to keep them away from her. Until she forgave herself, their history would remain an impediment. "What good would it have done me to stay bitter?"

"So you *were* bitter then."

"I was hurt. You didn't only leave town, you left me." Dealing with the false accusations had been easier than accepting the fact that Meg hadn't wanted him. Perhaps he never had accepted it.

"I wouldn't have been any good for you," she muttered.

"That's what we were told. I never believed it."

"But…" Her face was taut. "You had a future. Or you did, before I killed it."

"That wasn't intentional." There was only the slightest doubt in his voice. How the fire had started was one question he needed answered. For the book, but mostly for himself.

She didn't respond.

"I *know* it wasn't." He gentled his voice. "You weren't nearly as bad as you wanted people to think."

"Right." She surveyed the barn with a desperation, as if raw timbers and dusty banners were more vital than reopening old wounds. "Next you'll claim that you thought of me fondly while artillery flew overhead."

"You're not responsible for my entire career in the army," he said. "I could have gotten out after my first stint was up. I chose not to."

"Why? It was— Every time I watched the news— I hated to think of you—" She stopped, squeezing her face and fists into knots until her voice burst through again. "It's been torture."

Her hands flew open. She anchored them between her legs. "That must seem weak and stupid to you, when you were the one going through the real hell. While there I was, free—"

Rio cut her off. "Were you? Really?"

Her eyes went dull. "No. I was a mess. It took me a long time to understand how big a mess I really was."

"I wish you hadn't disappeared. If we'd been able to talk it out back then, you wouldn't have had to bear so much guilt for *my* choice." He picked up her paddle hand.

She pulled away. "What're you doing?"

He nodded toward the ring. "That's a good horse. You just opened the bidding."

Meg snapped back to the present, where one of the first horses they'd looked at was being auctioned, a beautiful prospect she couldn't afford. She shook her head even as she raised the paddle. "I'll never get this one."

She was right. The price on the black swiftly moved beyond her reach. But at least she'd regained her composure.

"This is not going well." She shifted around on the wooden bleacher, scanning the other bidders with a jaundiced eye. "The horses I can afford are going to the dog-food man and everyone else is after the ones that I actually want."

"Patience," Rio counseled.

Her eyes swiveled his way. She reminded him of Sloop, always watching him warily, keeping one step out of his reach. But he'd caught the horse and if necessary, he'd catch Meg, too.

"Patience," he repeated.

"That sounds familiar."

"Of course. You're still impetuous." She'd been the one to run into a flock of birds with her arms outspread. Eat her hot dog burned on one side and raw on the other. Concoct outrageous schemes one night and abandon them the next. Even though her desire to get away from Wild River hadn't flamed out like so many of her other plans, he'd always thought that they'd have more time together.

"At least that's a nicer way to put it. My dad would've just said I was unreliable." Meg drew in a breath. "And I guess he was right."

"He didn't know how to handle you.'

"Oh, ho. And you do?"

"I did once. I'm not so sure anymore."

She crossed her arms. "Someone's got to keep you on your toes."

He gestured to the ring. "What about this one?"

A young mare was up, prancing daintily on four white-stockinged hooves. She was a deep brown, almost black, with a beautiful head and arched neck.

Meg studied the mare longingly before checking the list. "Lot 112. Two years old, half Arab. Are you kidding?"

"Yes, but she's small, not a hair over fourteen-two." Any equine under fourteen-and-a-half hands at the withers was classified as a pony, each hand being four inches. "That'll limit the buyers. These cowboys and ranchers want size. Didn't you notice the parking lot?"

"There are plenty of other bidders," Meg said as the bidding ratcheted up. She joined in, flipping her paddle with a fatalistic air. When the price reached a thousand, she dropped out.

At twelve hundred, Rio liberated the paddle and made a bid.

"Hey!" she protested.

"I've got money."

"That's great. But since when were you in the market for a horse?"

"I'm not. We can be partners on her."

"Rio." Meg's voice was strangled. "Don't."

He hesitated. "What's the problem? The mare's an investment. Put a polish on her and you could sell her for triple the price next spring."

The auctioneer called for final bids. Rio made a motion, but Meg slapped the paddle down. "I don't want the complication of being partners."

"Going once, going twice," sang the auctioneer.

Rio looked at Meg. She gave him a tight-lipped profile.

"Going three times." The gavel banged. "Sold to the pretty lady in red!" A cute little blonde in a brightly colored cowboy hat clapped excitedly and threw her arms around a grinning older man, presumably her father, standing at the railing.

Rio dropped the paddle in Meg's lap. "Pardon me. I thought you'd be pleased."

"I don't need you to buy me things," she said. "And I definitely don't need a partner."

The words stung. He sat in silence as several horses were auctioned off.

"Let's go," she said at last. "There's nothing here for me."

"Not yet." Rio watched the ring without really seeing. He was turning Meg's reaction over in his mind. The vehemence had gone beyond her normal standoffishness. At the same time, he had to admit that he'd been presumptuous. He'd made too bold a move, too soon.

Especially considering that he wasn't quite certain what he'd do with her if he did choose to catch her.

You'd keep her, you fool.

A shrill whinny at the gate had every head turning. Lead rope trailing, the strawberry-roan mustang shot into the ring. She rocketed across the open space, flinging her heels in several wicked bucks. Dirt and sawdust flew.

Several of the auctioneer's men entered, spreading their arms to corner her. She jostled against them, lifting her nose with another frantic bugling call. An answer came from the holding ring.

"Her colt," Meg said from the edge of her seat. Some in the audience were chuckling, but she was anxious.

"Tempted?" asked Rio.

She shook her head with a grim resolution. "I don't need the trouble."

There were a few bids, but the interest in the mare remained lukewarm. The auctioneer joshed with the crowd, trying to work up a higher price, but the few bidders looked at the untamed mare and dropped out one by one. The man in the front row had the high bid.

"Going once," the auctioneer announced.

Meg said, "I have to," and raised her paddle.

The auctioneer nodded. "To you." He looked at the other bidder. "No? Going once…"

The slaughterhouse agent nodded. Meg immediately countered.

"Now we have an auction," the man at the podium said with relish. Meg's opponent upped his price, but her quick retaliation soon discouraged him. With disgust he dropped out of the bidding.

The cry of "Sold!" rang out. Meg sat back, apparently stunned to find herself the owner of an untamed mustang. Before she could absorb that reality, the colt was wrestled into the ring. It broke away from the handlers and bolted to his mother's side.

Meg let out a moan.

There was more interest in the colt. Several paddles went up as the bidding began. Meg sat unmoving.

Finally Rio nudged her. "You're not bidding?"

"What am I going to do with a colt?" She sat in silence, chewing her lip, then added, "Anyway, he needs to be weaned. They'd have to be kept apart. I don't have the space."

But her fingers squeezed the paddle handle compulsively as the auctioneer started his countdown. "Going once, twice…"

Do it, Rio thought. He had a fair idea of how much work the colt would be, but he also could tell that the wild-eyed, mistreated pair had some significance to Meg.

At the last second, her paddle shot up.

The gavel came down. "Mama and baby," the auctioneer said into the microphone, "sold to the lady with the sentimental heart." The audience laughed, turning to look up into the stands at Meg.

She glowered.

Rio had the smarts to keep his mouth shut.

THEY STOPPED for a late dinner at the Thunderhead Saloon, Treetop's favorite western-style roadhouse out on the highway east of town. The sky was dark and so was Meg's mood. She'd castigated herself for a good half hour after leaving the auction, giving in to her heart instead of listening with her head. Never a great idea.

"Well, hey, there, stranger," exclaimed the waitress, Ellen Molitor, a plain woman who'd been working at the Thunderhead for as long as anyone could remember. She'd come over with menus and a coffeepot after they'd seated themselves. "Rio Carefoot. Long time no see, darling." Ellen leaned down and gave him a loose one-armed hug. "And Meg. How's shakes, girl?"

Meg took a menu, offering only a noncommittal smile for an answer. She'd left under a black cloud and been away too long to feel at home among the townspeople, even the open-minded ones like Ellen. Not that anyone had brought up the past yet. To her face, anyway. But she knew they remembered.

Rio filled the gap. "Meg's shell-shocked. We're coming home from an auction in Laramie. She bought a couple of mustangs she hadn't planned on."

The waitress guffawed. "Caught the auction fever, huh? For me, it's yard sales. Other people's broken-down old junk. But my cabin's got to be furnished." She eyed Rio while she filled his cup. "What'd you get?"

He indicated the cowboy hat hung off the knob of the ladder-back chair. "Only a hat from one of the vendors."

"Nice. Guess ya gotta cowboy up now that you're home." Ellen took their orders, then gave Rio's shoulder a pat before she departed. "Welcome back, soldier."

"Hail the conquering hero," Meg said, her voice sounding a little hollow. "Seems like a lot of people have missed you. The town must resent me for sending you away."

"You didn't send me away. I wasn't rotting in jail, either. I spent one night there. It could have been worse, considering there was supposed to be a witness who saw me at the Vaughns' barn."

"Same difference. I was at fault."

"Nobody else but you knows that for sure."

"But they—" Meg gestured in general at the faces populating the roadhouse's tables and booths "—they know you wouldn't have been in trouble in the first place if it wasn't for me. Probably a lot of them have figured out that you were only protecting me. *I* was the one with the reputation."

"It was ten years ago, Meg. Why would they still remember, or care, even if they did?"

She scanned the large L-shaped room. A long bar ran along the wall and already there were customers bellied up with their beers, mostly men in jeans and jackets with their hats pulled low. The coat hooks and restrooms were tucked away in the hook of the L. A couple of women stood in line there, shooting looks at Meg and Rio and whispering behind their hands.

Gossip. "You're wrong. They do remember."

He turned his cup around on the saucer, hooking a finger through the handle. "I think it's you who can't forget."

She lowered her voice. "Do you think I should be able to forget what I did to you?" Her head hunched toward her shoulders. She was miserably aware of the eyes upon them. "I can't, Rio. Even though you're okay with it. If you really are."

He remained calm. When she was a girl, her adventurousness had always been a safe risk because she'd known there would a place to land with Rio. No wonder the decade without him had gone so wrong.

"If my life was ruined," he said evenly, "somebody forgot to tell me."

She narrowed her eyes. Although he hid his emotions well, she *knew* him. There had to be an inner turmoil going on. If she wasn't as bad as she pretended, he wasn't as good.

"Don't give me that," she scoffed. "You could have done something with yourself. You might have been a lawyer or a businessman or I don't know what. Someone important."

"Thanks, but I feel important enough."

"That's not what I meant to say. It's…" She searched. "Success, then. You could have money. Prominence. Respect."

"Those are fine things. But they're not the only components of success."

"You're out of step with the world."

"There's nothing wrong with that, Meg. You are too, living the simple life on the ranch."

"Yeah, but that's only 'cause I didn't have any other choice but coming home."

"Everything's a choice. Like the way I chose to take the blame for the fire when the deputy came to question me. I knew the consequences, Meg, but I did it because I wanted to protect you. I loved you."

An acrid thickness welled up inside her chest, pushing tears into her throat, her eyes. She took a deep breath, digging her fingernails into her palms. "I appreciate that, Rio. Really, I do. But I wish you'd told them the truth."

"I didn't know the truth. You were gone."

That night, after she'd fought with her father, Rio had found her hiding out in the barn. He'd begged her not to leave. When she hadn't been able to explain why she had to, he'd left her there, her hands shaking so badly she couldn't light her cigarette until the third try.

"Yeah," she said with a sigh. "I found out what you'd done weeks later, after you'd already appeared in front of the judge. If I'd known how much trouble you were in, I would've come back."

But would she have, really? On the road with one of her old boyfriends who'd promised to get her to Vegas, she'd felt free for the first time, even of Rio, the anchor who'd held her down.

That night, she'd divested herself of everything. She hadn't counted the cost until much later.

"You were with Addamo." Rio sounded, for him, bitter. Kris Addamo had been the most persistent of the boys who'd lured her away from Rio.

"He had a car that could get me out of town." Meg had pushed the girl she'd been then out of her mind. Looking back now, she could see how desperation had made her heartless. She'd used men and discarded them. But treated herself no better, if that counted for anything.

Rio looked as if he wanted to ask her the questions he'd asked that night. *Why? Wasn't he enough?*

She still couldn't answer.

She'd been scarcely eighteen years old, dealing with

a very private trauma. The sense of abandonment and loss had been too much for her to handle. Not even Rio—the one person who could have helped—had known what she was going through.

He would have given up everything for her if she'd asked him to, including his future. And that was why she hadn't. But then he'd ended up doing it anyway, by taking the blame for burning down the Vaughns' barn. If only he hadn't been so damn noble!

She looked around the busy bar and grill again before putting her head down. "This isn't the place for this conversation."

"Better than nothing," he said. "I'm counting myself lucky that you're talking to me at all."

"Huh! You're the one who's been the hermit, disappearing into the bunkhouse every time I turn around."

"Isn't that what you wanted?"

Rio…being evasive. While he certainly knew how to keep his feelings to himself, he'd never been sly or deceptive. If she asked, he'd answer. Most of the time, she hadn't asked. Because she hadn't really wanted to know.

Don't ask, don't tell, don't pass go.

Meg looked for their waitress. It seemed like hours since they'd sat down. "Just because this is a business relationship doesn't mean we can't be…"

Rio raised his eyebrows. The longer she hesitated about answering, the more his smile spread. Finally he said it for her. "Friends?"

"Cordial," she corrected, then turned her face aside to keep herself from showing too much relief. She pressed her lips together. The prospect of feeling easy around Rio again was so right and so fundamentally necessary that she was almost afraid to agree. She'd screwed up too many times.

"Okay," she blurted. "Friends. We'll try to be friends."

She doubted that it would be as easy as he might think, but they could try.

He offered his hand. "Friends."

She reached across the table to shake, but pulled her hand free as quickly as possible, covering her qualms with the arrival of their food. She pushed around the dishes and unrolled her silverware, asking Ellen for steak sauce and an extra napkin.

She could be friends with Rio. Maybe.

The real problem came in being *only* friends.

CHAPTER SIX

"IF IT AIN'T the fire starter."

Rio's head snapped up from the bucket he'd been rinsing with a hose that snaked from the barn's interior. An early cold snap had frozen the water. The rims of ice he'd pried free lay in shattered pieces on the muddy ground.

"Carefoot," his adversary said with a grunt. Behind the man, the doors to the delivery van hung open. Meg had rushed over to unload the mustangs, thrilled by their arrival even though she'd been swearing they'd be more trouble than they were worth.

"Yes?" Rio said warily.

The driver was bearded and burly in worn denim and a beat-up cowboy hat. His piggish eyes squinted at Rio. "Uh-huh. Thought that was you." He planted his boots and folded his arms across his chest. "Fire starter."

Rio straightened. "Excuse me?"

The driver's mouth pulled into a sneer. "That was my uncle's barn you burned."

Rio shook out the bucket and placed it on the ground. "The fire was an accident."

"You got proof of that?"

He chose his words carefully. "The investigators made a ruling. The cause of the fire was accidental. No accelerants were found."

The driver scowled. "Convenient for you, heh?"

Rio said nothing. Meg had gone still, standing at the edge of the heavy metal ramp. The other deliveryman walked up it with rattling footsteps. She motioned to him.

"Ya got nothing to say?" The driver paused. "Guess not. Same as in court."

Heat licked at Rio's nerve endings. "I didn't get your name."

There was another moment's hesitation. "Mitch Vaughn."

"Rio Carefoot."

No hands were offered. Vaughn stamped a boot heel. "Listen up, Carefoot. It's what I said. The Double V is owned by my uncle and aunt. Right down the road from here." He cocked his head in an easterly direction. "Looks like *somebody's* got too close for comfort and maybe *somebody* should be thinking of moving on. Know what I mean?"

"Have the Vaughns got a problem with me being here?"

"They're old. But they ain't defenseless. If you step one foot on Double V land..." Vaughn pointed his finger like a gun. "You'll get what you had coming ten years ago. If you're lucky, they'll only be firing buckshot."

"That's enough." Meg charged forward. "I know you, Mitch Vaughn. You think you're tough. But don't you dare come on my ranch and threaten my employee. It's only making you look like a fool, because you have no idea what you're saying."

She was up in his face, her hands knotted, but Vaughn wouldn't back down. "I'm saying he's a criminal. I don't give criminals second chances."

"That's not up to you."

Rio caught Meg's arm before she threw a punch. "Hey. It's okay."

She whirled on him. "It's *not* okay."

"The man said his piece. He had a right to it." Rio nodded at Vaughn. "I promise you, your aunt and uncle will have no trouble from me."

Meg was outraged. "Why should you take that from him? You didn't even do it!"

"He confessed," Vaughn jeered. "You can't get any guiltier than that."

"The fire was an accident," Meg said. "Rio—" She glanced at him. Her chin trembled. "Rio only took responsibility for it."

"Wasn't an accident that he was trespassing," Vaughn insisted.

"That's right." Rio calculated that Meg was on the verge of admitting her involvement. There was nothing to be gained by that except the relief of her guilt. Not a small consideration, but there would be a better way.

"I made a mistake and I paid for it," he continued.

He put his hand on her shoulder, prodding her toward the horse trailer. "So let's all just calm down and see if we can get these horses unloaded without any more fuss."

"Fuss," Meg said under her breath as Vaughn reluctantly joined his partner and undid the tail guard. The heavy metal snaps dropped with a clang against the partition. "Narrow-minded, hotheaded, bigmouthed—"

"Let it go, Meg. It's not worth it."

She blinked. "How can you stand it—having everyone believe you're guilty?"

"There are worse things."

"But how—"

He prodded her again. "Go tend to your mare."

The mustang came backing out of the trailer with her hind legs splayed and front hooves stamping a flamenco on the ramp. She tossed her head and whinnied shrilly. Vaughn yanked at the halter rope.

Meg ripped it from his grip. She used both hands to hold tight as the mare pulled back, shying and switching her tail. The second man backed out the colt. The pair of them rushed together, whickering and snorting reassurances, nose to nose. Meg's face relaxed.

Vaughn produced a clipboard and asked for her signature, still keeping his narrowed eyes on Rio. "We need the halters back."

"Wouldn't dream of keeping them," Meg snapped.

Rio led both horses to the round pen he'd been reinforcing the past few days. The mare was leery of passing through the gate, but once her colt was in she bolted after him.

Rio slipped off the halters and handed them to Vaughn while the younger man secured the ramp.

Meg stared at Vaughn with her hands on her hips. "We're done?"

Her starch was an admirable thing. Indefatigable, for the most part. Rio could understand why the guilt over not taking responsibility for the arson had eaten away at her. He would have to see if there was some way to help her out there.

Vaughn smiled unpleasantly. "We're done."

"Go on, then."

She didn't watch them depart. After a minute, Rio joined her at the tall fence of the round pen. She was brooding, her chin on her hands, her eyes following the mare and colt as they strutted around the enclosure, checking out their temporary home. Since mustangs were accustomed to roaming free, they tended to shy away from indoor box stalls. Getting the horses used to their new, domesticated life would be a gradual process.

The youngster lifted his nose and squealed at the sight of the strange horses in the neighboring corrals that extended from the barn. The three of them crowded the railing. Curious creatures.

"Look at the tail on that colt," Rio said. It was spinning like a propeller.

"Ought to call him Whirligig." Meg laughed. "It's been a long time since there was a baby on the ranch."

"What about a puppy? Wouldn't you like a puppy?"

Something in her expression closed down. "What's with the dog hang-up? I think it's *you* who wants one."

"Maybe." He had wanted a dog as a kid. But he'd never been allowed. He'd even begged, certain that his mother could persuade Mr. Stone to make an allowance, but she'd been staunch about letting Rio know that they were employees at the ranch, not family. She'd said that he could have a dog when they had their own place. But they'd never got either one.

Rio surveyed the barn, the pastures, the small cabin perched above the river. This wasn't his place either, even though he was coming to feel at home. His uneasiness had to do with Meg herself.

What if he fell back in love with her, only to end up rejected again?

"If you want a dog," she said reluctantly, "I suppose that'd be all right. So long as you take care of it."

"We'll see."

She shot him a look. "Nothing upsets you."

"You're talking about Vaughn?"

"He's a jerk."

"How come I don't remember him?"

"He's older than us. Ten or fifteen years." Meg's lips curled with distaste. "But not so old that he didn't once offer to buy me beer and cigarettes if I'd go for a ride with him in his pickup truck." She scoffed. "A *ride*. Right. I was only sixteen, but not naive."

Rio clenched his hands. Slowly he opened them,

stretching his fingers wide. "I guess it's a good thing you didn't tell me that earlier."

She pushed away from the sturdy board fence. "Listen. I've been thinking and…I could come clean about the fire. All I'd have to do is confide in one person. It wouldn't take long before the whole town would know. Then your name would be cleared. Not in a court of law, but it'd be something."

"Don't do it for my sake."

"Why not? Don't you care when some idiot like Vaughn insults you?"

"His kind can't hurt you unless you let them." He brushed her hair off her shoulders. The strands slipped through his fingers like corn silk. "His insults are water off a duck's back. You might want to try that sometime."

She sighed. "I'll never be so easygoing."

"That's okay. I kind of enjoy it when you're riled."

"Yeah?"

He leaned against the pen, one leg crossed over the other, his arms folded. He hadn't touched her often in the couple of weeks he'd been here, but he remembered each time. A hand on her elbow when she climbed into his pickup. Brushing by her in a box stall. Their fingers touching when they'd both plunged a sponge into a bucket of sudsy water at the same time.

Alone in bed at night, he imagined what she would do if he tried to kiss her.

"Yeah," he said.

Her cheeks pinked up. Maybe she'd read his thoughts.

She moved away, saying brusquely, "Well, if you don't get back to work, you'll have the opportunity to see me get real riled."

"Yes, Sarge."

She stomped off to the barn. "And quit calling me Sarge!"

MEG WORKED with the mustangs all afternoon, doing nothing much except grooming and haltering them, letting them get used to her. She'd painted their raw wounds and rubbed liniment into the mare's scarred hide, crooning and clucking all the while until Rio had said that she sounded like a broody old mother hen, watching over her chicks.

"Go and get your puppy," she'd retorted, "and then we'll see who's the bigger sap."

She'd just about died over her unthinking remark about there being no babies on the ranch. No matter how lonely she got or how empty she felt, she couldn't let Rio get the idea she wanted babies—of any sort.

Not chicks or foals or…or…puppies.

She didn't say a lot during dinner, taking a book to the table and reading it—or pretending to read it, since she couldn't seem to make it past page three—over her plate of country-fried ham and hash browns.

"I've been thinking," Rio said, getting up to clear. He cut into the applesauce cake she'd made from a mix.

She kept her nose in the book. "Never do that. It only leads to trouble."

"I've been thinking about the Vaughns."

She squeezed her eyes shut, just for a millisecond. "Because of that jerk, I suppose."

Rio put a cake plate in front of her, nudging aside her book. "I should go over there, say hello. It's the right thing to do."

"Say hello," she repeated.

"They're owed an apology. Even if it's way too late." He stood beside the table, calmly sipping from a coffee mug.

She ran her gaze up him, a lump in her throat even before she reached his eyes. Why did he have to be so honorable? That had been the thing with Rio, even as a boy. He'd held himself to high standards and he'd acted as if she would naturally do the same.

She'd let him down, over and over. That had hurt worse than never meeting her father's expectations. Although Rio had not once rebuked her, she'd seen the disappointment in his eyes. When she'd left early from a football game in some boy's car. Or cut class to go smoke in the woods with the potheads.

He'd wanted to love her, and she'd wanted something else, something she'd never been able to define. She'd only known it wasn't the ranch.

Yet here she was, full circle.

"Would you come with me?" he asked. "To the Vaughns'?"

She blanched. Yep. Here she was, disappointing him again.

"I can't," she said, bolting from the table.

Dashing through the dining room, she slammed her hip into the corner of her mother's china cabinet. The fragile dishes rattled.

Tears of pain sprang to Meg's eyes. "Stupid dishes," she snapped, amazed her father had kept them around. Dusty, unused relics of another era, when her mother had come to the ranch with a frilly trousseau and a truckload of impractical wedding gifts. Royal Doulton china. Silver service for eight. Ginger jars and incense burners, as if any of it had a place on a ranch.

Her mother hadn't belonged, either.

Meg stared at the dishes, transfixed even though Rio might appear at any moment. At one time, she'd believed her parents' love story was romantic. From the outside looking in, anyway. Small-town beauty queen Jolene Batinkoff had married taciturn cowboy Richard Lennox despite her parents' disapproval. They'd hated the thought of their only daughter going off to live on a remote ranch in Wyoming. They'd been right. She hadn't been suited to the rigors of rural life.

Jolene had told tales of her early years on the ranch, making her travails sound comic and lighthearted— bedtime stories for little Meg. Mother and daughter had cut paper dolls and planned tea parties, but as Meg had grown it had become clear that she was truly her father's daughter, more interested in riding and ranch work than indoor activities. Gradually Jolene's depression had deepened until there'd been only one way out.

Meg got moving again, into the living room. She

dropped onto the sofa. Took a deep breath. She wasn't going to lose it over faded memories of her broken-down mother. And definitely not over a proposed trip to the neighbors'. She wasn't going, either, but she didn't have to show Rio she cared. Or was scared. Not of a kind, elderly couple like the Vaughns.

Rio had followed her through the dining room. She looked up. He stood in the open doorway, holding his cowboy hat. "Think about it?"

Her face was hot, but she shrugged. "Sure."

"Just a friendly visit."

"Mmm."

"I'd appreciate the company. The Vaughns might, too." Rio's head tilted. "I don't suppose you've seen them since you've been back?"

"Nope."

"They're good people."

"I know." She stared out the picture window. *But I'm not.*

A HEAVY THUD OUTSIDE jarred Meg awake. She sat up in bed and pushed her hair out of her eyes, trying to place the sound. A tree branch falling. The high-altitude wind could be especially bad this time of year. But she didn't hear it, not even the low moaning sigh that was almost constant, come autumn.

The house was drafty. She slid under the covers, hoping she'd fall back asleep. She'd turned in early so that she wouldn't have to think. Or crave.

Bad sign. She ran a finger across the inside of her wrist. A counselor had told her that her problems with substance abuse were another form of running away. And that running away was a symptom of her abandonment issues. That made some sense, but big deal. There were no solutions.

Not even coming home had helped a whole lot, because she was alone here, too. Rio wasn't *staying*.

Thunk.

That one was close. Meg jumped out of bed. The blind went up with a snap, but her window faced the river and the mountains. The thuds were coming from the other side of the house.

She *could* see the bunkhouse. The light was still on.

Almost 1:00 a.m. Did Rio never sleep? What was he doing in that cabin?

She heard two more thudding sounds, right on top of each other. She stepped into the jeans she'd dropped on the floor, zipping them as she headed for the front door. Was that a car door opening?

A loud bang made her flinch. Something had hit the porch—probably a rock.

"Kids," she said, but there was a pit in her stomach.

Next came the rev of an engine, an incoherent, jeering insult. Headlights flashed through the windows.

She switched on the lights. Let them know she was up, give them a chance to get away because she was, suddenly, more afraid than outraged.

At the foyer, she yanked on a pair of boots. Instead

of throwing open the front door where she could hear a vehicle in the driveway, she went along the hallway to her father's study. Her teeth hurt from gritting them. Since moving home, she'd been in the room only a few times, gathering necessary tax or insurance papers. Her father's presence was too strong.

Another rock hit the porch roof and rolled off. Moving quickly, she turned on a lamp, found the keys in a desk drawer.

She opened the gun cabinet.

RIO WAS ALREADY HALFWAY to the house when the sharp crack of a single shotgun fire sent him diving for the earth. The ground seemed to rise up to meet him. Hard as concrete. The air left his lungs with a grunt. He was on his feet in the next instant, running now.

Meg was alone up at the house.

He skidded to a stop at the edge of the porch. Meg stood on the steps, shotgun held upright against one cocked hip. Red brake lights blinked at the end of the driveway as a vehicle turned onto the main road, roaring off to the accompaniment of the clatter of tossed beer cans.

Meg was the widow in every western made, defending her homestead. "What the hell?"

"It was nothing." She was cracking the shotgun, sliding out the unspent shells. "Joyriders," she said calmly. "Throwing rocks."

"Vaughn, you think?"

She frowned, her face deeply shadowed by the porch roof. "I don't know. It was a pickup truck. That's all I saw."

"Could have been anyone then."

A ghost of a grin moved across her mouth. "Used to be me. That was the kind of stupid trick I once thought was cool and rebellious."

Aware of the cold now, he crossed his arms, hands in his armpits. "You okay?"

Her hair swung forward as she turned away. "Of course." She was slim in a clinging long-sleeved tee and unsnapped jeans that showed a triangle of flat belly and the puckered waistband of a pair of flannel pajama pants.

She set the rifle inside the open door. "Want to come in and get warm?"

He toed the jamb with an unlaced boot. He couldn't remember putting them on.

Meg's gaze lifted to his face. "You never went to bed."

"Not because I was expecting this." He motioned to the road.

"It was probably kids," she reiterated. "I scared 'em off. No reason to involve the cops."

"Hmm. I suppose not."

She moved into the crowded entryway. Every light was on in the house. "Coffee?"

"That'll wake us up more."

"Hot chocolate, then."

"No. It's late. I should go back." He reached for the door. "Unless you don't feel safe."

Meg's chin went up. "I'm fine. They threw a few rocks, that's all."

"Childish stuff for a man as old as Vaughn." Rio moved inside the doorway, just far enough to close it and keep the heat in. He wasn't staying.

"That's why it was probably teenagers."

"Why would they…?"

She shrugged. "I didn't remember having any great motive. Just restlessness, boredom. My dad called it high jinks. He might even have approved if I'd been a son."

She hadn't stepped away. The foyer seemed more crowded than ever, filled with jackets and tools and too much Meg. Rio could smell the sleep on her, but her green eyes were as clear and sharp as a shard from a beer bottle.

He looked away. Being alone with her on the ranch was always going to be difficult, but he felt the pull of her particularly at night. Too many memories of Meg came to him in the dark.

Once, well past midnight, she'd showed up at the Stone ranch after a date with one of her boyfriends, a football jock who'd already bragged in the locker room about making out with her. She'd tapped on Rio's bedroom window, asking to be let in.

That had been twelve years ago, when he was just seventeen. But he remembered all too well the strange brightness of her eyes and the energy pulsating from her as she prowled around the room, looking at this and that, picking up books, putting them down, studying the posters on the wall as if she'd never seen them before, as if every item in the room was new. Including him.

She'd jumped onto the bed, beside him, and cradled his pillow to her chest as she talked about everything except her date. How boring and provincial Treetop was. How much she resented her father's rules. How she was going away after graduation, if she could wait that long, to a city where there'd be doormen at the apartment buildings, shrimp cocktail served fresh, limos and bright lights and men who wore tuxedos instead of jeans and boots.

Rio had tried to listen but he'd been consumed with the plumpness of her recently kissed mouth, the swish of her hair, the female scent that rose from her warm, flushed skin. When finally her energy had run down, she'd stretched out beside him, given him a friendly hug and whispered that he wouldn't mind if she stayed over, would he, if she promised to sneak out at dawn so he wouldn't get into trouble?

He'd had to turn away so she wouldn't know how aroused he'd been. Or see that he'd ached for her, even though they'd agreed that they were better off as friends than a romantic couple. Her idea.

His torture.

Rio cleared his throat, focusing on this night, not the ones that were done and gone, having gotten him nowhere but in trouble. "Uh, do you have any enemies?"

Meg flicked a hand. "Only if someone is nursing a very old grudge."

"Which brings us back to Vaughn."

"Forget it. No harm done."

"You were fast with that shotgun. That could be, you know, dangerous."

"I shot into the air, just a warning. They knew that." She watched him searchingly. "You should have a gun down at the cabin, just in case. To scare away coyotes or bear."

He'd barely grunted when she added, "Unless…do you have, um, problems? What's that thing—PSTD?"

"PTSD." Post-traumatic stress disorder. "I'm all right, Meg."

"If you suffer nightmares…?" she suggested cautiously. "Seems like your light is always on."

"I've had nightmares. But it's been a while. No worries. No memories I can't handle."

Unless he counted the memories of her.

"Well, my dad—he was in Nam and he never got over it completely. I don't know if he had nightmares, but I learned real young that I couldn't wake him suddenly, or walk up behind him, without startling us both." She shuffled her feet. Glanced up at Rio before bending to slip out of her boots. "You're sure you don't want coffee?"

He let his gaze linger over the line of her back, the fuller curves of her backside. He jammed his hands into the pockets of his jeans, then took them out just as hastily when the motion pulled his fly taut against the swelling of his groin.

"Do you think about your father often?" he asked gruffly.

He knew he should go. She was getting the wrong idea about him, casting him in the role of the traumatized vet.

Then again, maybe she wasn't entirely wrong. While he might not be up with nightmares, that was only because he'd found a better way to work things out— through writing. He'd done good work the past week. Good enough that he had to continue even if he was risking his relationship with Meg, with his mother, with the man who'd never earned the title of father.

"Do I think of my father?" Meg had straightened. She drew back her hair, twisting it into a loose knot around her hand. She flung it past her shoulders, making a face. "Nope. Not if I can help it."

"He deserves your respect."

"Does he?" Her expression darkened. "He didn't even want me at his funeral, you know."

Rio winced. That was harsh, but Richard Lennox had been a harsh man. "Have you been to his grave?"

"Yeah. Once. He's buried beside my mom." She shivered. "God, this is gruesome talk for the middle of the night. I'll never get back to sleep." She contemplated him. "Will you?"

Her voice was rough velvet. Rio felt it as surely as if she'd brushed up against him.

"I'd better," he said gruffly. "The horses'll be waking me before too long."

She barely nodded. Her hair hung loose against her face again, making him remember how she'd looked that one special night, how her hair had fallen between them like a veil as she climbed on top of him in his narrow bed, her eyes huge, glistening with the knowledge that he wanted her.

She'd put her hand on him. The shock of pleasure had been as intense as a thunderbolt. He'd blurted that he loved her. He'd always loved her. But she'd laughed, as if she knew better. That what he was feeling was lust.

Months after becoming lovers, she'd wanted to break up. See other guys. Their romantic relationship had been off and on after that, off whenever Meg had found someone new, on when she'd decided that different wasn't better after all. Each time, he'd tried to resist. Each time, he'd failed.

Rio had been telling himself that he was different now. Stronger. More confident. Resistant to her.

He had to nudge against her to make room to open the door. She didn't fall back, and for one tick of the clock they were pressed against each other. That, he thought, would be the beat his heart skipped. All sensation, every pulse, had dropped to the straining thickness of his erection.

And then the moment was over. He was safely outside, sucking the cold, bracing air into his constricted lungs. "See you in the morning," he said before closing the door between them.

CHAPTER SEVEN

"RIO!" MEG BURST INTO the bunkhouse with an armful of fresh towels. "I've got a job."

He wasn't there. She'd known that, at the back of her mind. That morning, he'd said something about checking out what kind of shape the haymow was in, making ready for a delivery of the alfalfa they'd need to see the stock through the winter. He'd also mentioned a cat. That every barn needed a good mouser. He'd ask around town. Someone was always giving away kittens.

She looked around the cabin. Little had changed since he'd moved in after their first, thorough cleaning.

Rio was neat. He had been even before the military, she recalled. His small room at the Stone ranch had always been tidy, almost as if no one had lived there. A poster or two on the walls, his books on the desk.

She ducked down to glance under the bed, smelling the clean scent of the towels pressed to her chest. Only a duffel bag, empty, by the flattened look of it.

The bedsprings squeaked as she sat. Dust motes

danced in the shaft of afternoon sunlight cast through the small window. She felt a draft at the back of her neck.

Was he warm enough? One of her mother's old quilts was spread across the bed, with a couple of extra wool blankets folded at the foot. There was the wood stove, too, an orderly stack of hardwood nearby. Rio had sharpened her father's ax and chain saw and had been hauling, cutting and splitting the ranch's dead and fallen trees. Meg was adept at that chore, too, but she had to admit there was something about having a competent man around that warmed her. Something that went beyond the obvious attraction offered by flexing muscles and on-display virility.

She'd learned to value his caring. His protectiveness. Far more than she had as a teenager.

Meg put the towels down. She was an independent woman. Had made quite a proclamation of that, in fact. But she had known what it was like to be cared for. Her last long-term relationship had been with Jase Camillo, who'd found her at a low point and literally saved her life. They'd been together for three years.

But she'd mistaken concern and caring for love. When she'd learned she was pregnant, the truth had come out. Jase didn't want to marry her. She was too damaged. Not good enough to be his wife.

Meg looked down at her hands. The tattooed bracelets around her wrists. She tugged her sleeves over the designs. She didn't have to rub them to feel the thin scars they concealed.

"Don't," she whispered. *Don't do this to yourself.*

Her life might not be better, not yet, but it was a life. Today, there was even optimism.

Meg stood, the image of Rio in her mind, and walked over to the desk. She ran her fingers along the spines of novels and nonfiction, a small collection bookended by a thick thesaurus and dictionary. Hmm.

The lamp. A laptop. A printer. And a sheaf of papers, turned so the writing was facedown. She thumbed the corners of the pages.

Don't look.

No, look.

What he's doing in here is none of your business. His private time is his own.

But I'm curious, she argued. *One peek won't hurt.*

She opened the laptop, but it was shut down. She didn't have the temerity to actually power up and search his files. Her attention went back to the pages, her fingers hovering above them.

One glance.

She picked up the top sheet and read the scribbled notation at the bottom of a page of printing, dated a couple of days ago: *A tour of Afghanistan. Sounds like a tourist trip. If so, I don't recommend the meal plan.*

A smile teased at the corners of her mouth. Until she glanced at the rest of the page. Then she began reading in earnest about a sniper attack that ended with a short but searing image of blood and pain and terror.

She reached with shaking hands for another page, fumbled with the pile and pulled one out at random.

Meg Lennox. How do I describe Meg? When I first knew her, she was as shy as a newborn filly, nothing but big eyes and long wobbly legs.

Meg was suddenly swirling at sea, as if a wave had crashed over her. Her heart was heavy and sinking fast.

Rio was writing.

He was writing about her.

She heard a sound outside and tried to straighten the pile of paper. She put the top sheet back in place. The edges were creased. She must have held it too tightly.

The door opened. Rio scraped his boots on the step before entering. His eyebrows shot up. "Meg."

"I brought clean towels," she said, knowing all the color had leached out of her face. She took a big sideways step toward the bed, avoiding his gaze. He wasn't fooled.

He walked to the desk and saw the wrinkled page. With a thud, he dropped the dictionary on top of the pile.

"I'm sorry," she blurted. "I was curious about what you do out here, all alone."

His eyes rose to hers. A piercing stare. "What did you discover?"

"You're writing." She licked her lips. "About the war. About me."

"It's only…" He shrugged. "Yes. It's a memoir. Maybe going to be one, I guess. I'm not sure yet."

"Oh. Well. That's…" Words were sticky in her mouth. "Surprising. I didn't know."

"It started as a blog, while I was on duty."

Her eyes widened questioningly.

"Now it might be a book."

"A book?" she echoed faintly.

And she didn't yet know the full extent of what that meant. But he couldn't hide anymore, so he said bluntly, "I have interest from New York."

"What does that mean?"

"There's a literary agent who represents me. She's waiting for pages right now."

Meg flopped down on the bed as if her legs could no longer hold her. "That's huge. It's amazing. Why didn't you tell me?"

"There's nothing certain yet. The whole thing could come to nothing."

"It won't," she said, her voice as raw as grated knuckles. "But…"

"You want to know if you'll be in the book."

She looked ashamed. "I saw my name."

"I can give you a fictional one." Said with some reluctance.

"To protect the guilty?"

The fire, her running away—although those things had changed the course of their lives, they didn't define her for him. She couldn't see that now. Was it hubris to think that reading his version of their relationship might change that for her?

He swallowed. "You're a big part of my life. My early life, anyway." And now his present. Perhaps even his future. "I can't leave you out."

She stood and walked to the window, staring blankly at the turbulent river, several shades darker than the slate-gray sky. Her chest heaved. "Even if you change my name, everyone in Treetop will know it's me."

"Yeah."

She pressed her palms to the glass. Spread her fingers. "Punishment," she whispered.

"No," he said. "I promise—it won't be like that. I'm not out to get people." But something snaked inside his gut. Telling the truth would accomplish the same result, as surely as if he'd purposely set out for revenge. His mother didn't deserve that. Nor Meg, even if she thought she did.

As for his father…

Rio's book could blow the roof off Stone ranch.

Meg must have been thinking in the same direction. She was one of the few people who knew what Rio had learned at age sixteen. That William Walker Stone, former state senator and wealthy married rancher, had fathered an illegitimate child by his Crow Indian house-keeper.

Meg turned and looked at him warily. Her mouth opened. At first no words came out, but he could see what she wanted to say. Concern for him had softened her own instinct for self-preservation.

"Your father," she said. "What about him?"

Rio stiffened. "I don't call him that. He wasn't a father."

"No, but there's more between you than biology."

Down deep, he knew she was right. The book might be his way of acknowledging that. Still, he shook his head. "I'm not going to worry about what Stone thinks. He can take care of himself."

"But your mother—"

"She's against the book."

"Then she knows about it."

"Yes, but we're at a standstill over it. I don't want to cause her grief, but that's exactly what'll happen if I actually manage to get published."

"You don't have to tell every secret."

He cocked his head. Meg's arms were crossed and her expression was blank, closed. Was she thinking of his family's reputation…or hers?

"Then it wouldn't be much of a memoir."

"Isn't your war experience the big sell? Why should the general public, outside of Treetop, care about your parentage and your childhood and all the rest of it?" Meg's voice had started out low, but rose until she ended on a chirp. Not like her. She was really bothered.

That gave Rio a qualm, but for once he wasn't going to give in. Ten years ago, he'd let too many things go, in the interest of keeping the peace between them.

"Maybe they don't care, but I do." He hadn't started with the intention of working through his feelings by writing them out, but that's what was happening. He laid his hand on the desk. "This is important to me."

"More important than the people you—" Color flared in her face. "People you care about."

"Maybe it's time for those people to show some caring for me and what I need. For a change."

Meg circled the bed. "You don't think I have?"

"Have you? Ever?"

Her expression hardened for a moment, then crumpled like tissue paper. Her mouth thinned. "I guess you're right," she muttered, brushing past him.

He caught her by the arm. "Meg, wait."

"No." She shook him off. "I've been a heartless witch with you and it's time I faced up to that. I probably even deserve to have you share that with the world."

Acid laced her every word. While Rio recognized that it was directed inwardly, he felt the sting.

"I'm sorry," he said as she opened the door. "I'm going to write my truth. All of it. The book may never be published. But it could be. Maybe in a different form, maybe not." He didn't move. He was letting her go. "I can't make any promises."

"I never did either." She glanced back, hugging herself from the cold in a thick hand-knitted sweater. "So it looks like we're even at last."

THEY DIDN'T SEE each other again until feeding time at the barn. Meg didn't speak. Rio wasn't inclined to, either, though he had no problem communicating with the horses like some sort of Doctor Dolittle, through clucks and hand strokes. The pair of mustangs had been moved to one of the corrals connected to the box stalls. The way he crooned and practically purred to them made her stomach flutter.

Meg got the hose that was attached to the barn's only indoor spigot and filled the water buckets. So what if he was ignoring her? Talking wasn't necessary. They had the routine down pat. The horses were already inside, except for the mustangs. They still hadn't entered their stall, though the Dutch door was always left open. They all munched on their ration of oats. Rio was doling out the flakes of hay.

This was what she'd wanted—a working relationship. And she couldn't stand it.

She forced herself to speak first. "I didn't have the chance to tell you. I got a new job." The words came easier once she was started. "Remember that half-Arab at the auction?"

Rio stepped out of Renny's stall. "Uh-huh."

Not much enthusiasm there, but only because he was treading lightly.

"The woman who bought the Arab called me this morning. Sloop's owner recommended me. She wants to board the horse here for the winter, let me work with the mare on my own, keeping her exercised mostly. And then in spring I'll up the training and give the owner riding lessons as she needs them."

Rio picked up another flake of hay, moving past her to the next stall. His eyes crinkled in an understated smile. "Nice going, Meggie Jo."

Relief flooded Meg. She told herself it was the release of finally getting to share her pent-up news. "The mare will be arriving tomorrow."

"Good. Keep it up and there might even be enough work around here to justify my paycheck."

"What do you mean by that? You've been doing plenty."

"Sure I have. But one person can care for five horses on her own, especially when it's a shoestring operation."

"Now there'll be six."

"Just the same…"

"I suppose I could handle the work, as long as I never wanted any time off. But it's not like I'm paying you a high salary."

He huffed in agreement as he slid open Sloop's door. "I was just wondering." He shook out the hay and filled the net. His dark eyes gleamed at her from the depth of the stall. "I even considered whether or not you were lonely out here and just wanted someone else around once in a while. But you've been pretty clear about that."

She didn't know how to react. Couldn't tell where he was going with what felt like a taunting probe. She aimed and squeezed the hose trigger. The strong blast of water into the bucket felt satisfying, even if half of it foamed out to splash over the concrete floor.

"If I wanted company, I'd find it."

Yeah, sure. Like old boyfriends? Any of them left in town had to be settled down by now. If they weren't, and still had their old habits, she wasn't going anywhere near them. She was trying like hell to keep on the straight and narrow.

Trying like heck.

"What's that smile for?" Rio asked.

"Can you imagine me making friends? Going shopping with the girls? Planning a church bake sale."

"It wouldn't hurt either of us to get involved in the community."

Meg heaved the bucket up and hung it on the hook in Sloop's stall. She hovered for a couple of seconds, picking flecks of straw off the chestnut's flank. "They don't need me." Or want me.

She was her father's daughter, after all.

She picked up the hose again and punched the trigger, accidentally on purpose spraying him.

With a confounded laugh, he stepped out of her way.

"Oops. *Sorry.*"

Rio's eyes followed her as she lugged the last bucket to the mustangs' unoccupied stall. He caught up and took it from her hand. "Congrats on the new client. I'm happy for you."

"Thanks." She rested her arms on the top of the partition, half hiding her face against the bulky sleeves of the sweater she'd found in a trunk in the master bedroom. "Things are looking up."

Aside from his news about the book.

But she didn't want to think about that right now, not when they were getting along.

"I'll be gone for dinner," Rio said abruptly from the

stall, where he'd set the water bucket just outside the Dutch door.

Meg bit the inside of her cheek. "Um. Okay."

"I should have mentioned it sooner."

"Doesn't matter."

He chirruped and said, "Gig," moving the curious colt along with a gentle hand. They'd begun calling him that, short for Whirligig. "Dinner with my mother."

"Fine." Meg burrowed deeper into her sleeved arms, until only her eyes showed, narrowed at him with suspicion. Had he arranged the dinner to get away from his shrew of a boss?

"We're going to the Thunderhead, if you wanted to join us."

She caught her breath. Held it. Released it. "Not this time," she said evenly.

"Then next time?"

No, thanks. For a distraction, she nodded at the wild mare, who was hovering at the door with her colt. She'd come to look inside, but she kept out of arm's reach. No one was trapping her in a box without an exit. "We need a name for the roan."

"Axxaashe," Rio said after a contemplative pause.

"What's that mean?"

"Crow for sun."

"Axxaashe. That's okay, but I don't get it. Why sun?"

He shrugged. "Just thought we both could use a little light in our lives."

The next day the limo arrived.

CHAPTER EIGHT

IT WASN'T ACTUALLY a limo, Meg realized at closer look. The car had stopped in front of the house. It was a large, polished, deluxe Cadillac, as alien to Wild River Ranch as a golf cart filled with plaid-trousered duffers. A driver got out, dressed sharply in black boots, jeans and a western shirt, topped by a bolo tie, black suede cowboy hat and sunglasses. Chauffeur, Wyoming style.

Meg slid off the saddle blanket she'd been running over Axxaashe's back and sides. Leaving the horse haltered and tied, she draped the blanket over the fence and ducked to climb through the railings.

The chauffeur had seen her. She acknowledged him with a nod, buying time by stopping to unwind her scarf. The hairs on her nape prickled. The chauffeur's head had inclined to talk to someone inside the car, but tinted windows hid the occupant.

This can come to no good, she thought. Meg pasted on a smile anyway as she approached the car. Might be a potential client.

She strode up the slope to the main driveway, her boots crunching on the thin gravel. She glanced into the barn as she passed. No sign of Rio, but he was there, shoveling out stalls. Never mind. She could handle this on her own.

"Miss Lennox?" the driver said. "Margaret Lennox?"

"That's right." Miss Lennox sounded like a name that belonged to a sweet kindergarten teacher. She'd never gone by Margaret either, so she brusquely added, "But it's Meg."

The driver opened the back door. A tall white-haired man emerged, wearing a tailored business suit that gave the impression of wealth and substance even though it hung from his frame. As if illness or age had stolen his former bulk.

The driver stood at attention beside the car door. "Mr. Stone would like to speak with you."

Stone. Meg stared, not caring if she appeared rude.

In person, she'd seen the former senator only from a distance. But his face had been everywhere during election season. He'd aged since then, of course. Grown more gaunt and lined. The dark eyes and uncompromising jaw were the same, the narrow-bridged nose more prominent. Almost hawkish. He'd always worn a cowboy hat in his commercials and literature, but now his head was bare.

The wind ruffled his thinning hair. His pink scalp showed through, which seemed oddly intimate to Meg, as if she'd glimpsed a vulnerability. "I'm Meg Lennox."

"Senator William Walker Stone." He extended his hand.

As Meg reached to take it, one sharp word carried from behind her, not loudly spoken but remarkably distinct.

"Shit."

It was Rio, standing at the door of the barn.

Stone's mouth creased into a narrow line. "Miss Lennox. I am told you are the proprietor of Wild River Ranch?"

"Uh-huh."

Stone scanned then dismissed the ranch as of no consequence. Meg's back went up, even though she knew her place was a mere pebble next to the Stone spread, which boasted thousands of acres of grazing land and a herd of cattle that was one of the largest in the state.

"You employ Rio Carefoot," the former senator said.

She cocked her head at Rio, who stood outside the barn with his arms folded. He was obviously staring daggers, even at this distance. "That's him." *And you know it.*

"Yes, it is." Even the authoritative Stone seemed subdued. He didn't actually look at Rio. "May I have your permission to speak with him?"

She blinked. "That's up to Rio. He's my employee, not my chattel."

"I don't wish to impede your…operations."

Meg almost snorted. As if Stone gave a damn about her operations. He was making a show of his power and authority. Making her complicit to whatever maneuver he was on to.

She was forestalled from blurting out an ill-advised comment by another passenger springing from the car. The visitor gave a piercing squeal. "Rio!"

Without so much as a glance at Meg, the woman bounded toward the barn, her arms outspread.

Melissa Stone, Meg surmised, although she didn't recognize Stone's daughter. The last time she'd seen Lissy, the girl had been a pretentious fourteen-year-old spending part of her summer vacation at the family ranch. She'd scorned Meg's shabby clothes and stringy hair, while openly admiring Rio, perhaps because he had been, on the surface, completely indifferent to her.

"Melissa," said Stone, using her name as a rebuke.

"Oh, be quiet, Daddy." Lissy threw herself into Rio's arms, even though he looked more stunned than welcoming.

"Lissy?" he said.

"Rio!" She kissed him emphatically on the cheek. "I can't believe it's you." A hug followed, her face pressed to his chest as she nestled against him even though she was only a few inches shorter in her high-heeled boots.

The cuddle seemed awkward to Meg, but what did she know? She'd gotten halfway to the barn and she couldn't remember taking a step. She stopped, realizing that Stone had followed her, while still not actually looking at Rio.

Look at him, Meg wanted to say. See him. Be proud of him!

She brushed a hand across her eyes. Rio wasn't

paying any attention to Stone, either, even though the tension between them was so thick it could have been buttered bread.

Rio held Lissy at arm's length, looking her up and down. As a teenager she'd been pimply and round, but now she was tall like her father, slim and well dressed, with pale hair the color of buttercream. Features a shade too sharp to be considered beautiful.

"You've grown up," he said.

She beamed. "So have you."

He pulled back and held his hands up to show her the grime. "Sorry. I've been cleaning the barn."

Lissy laughed. "I certainly don't care about smudges!" She surely did, but was clearly willing to tolerate them in his case.

She'd be thirty-four now, Meg estimated. Stone's oldest. Billy, her brother, had only been a year younger than Rio. A pudgy sandy-haired kid with freckles, who'd been either gung ho about their summertime friendship or selfish about his bike and his horses and his ranch. Annoying to Meg, either way. Back then, she'd preferred the company of Rio alone.

Lissy glanced over her shoulder, looking past Meg to her father. Her lips puckered. "Dad, won't you come see Rio?"

"Certainly."

This oughta be fun. If not for Rio, Meg would have felt some satisfaction in Stone's discomfort. How did a man greet the son he'd never acknowledged, especially after orchestrating the off-the-books agreement that had sent Rio to war instead of jail? That had been some choice "granted" by Stone, as if the man expected to be lauded for his generosity.

But there was no confrontation. Meg suspected Rio's calm hid a lifetime of emotion.

She'd seen how passionate he could be under the right circumstances—and been so young and foolish that she'd thrown it away.

The two men shook hands. They could have been strangers. Except a stranger wouldn't have turned Rio's eyes to flint.

"We need to talk," Stone said, skipping the polite preliminaries. Not even an "It's good to see you again."

Rio looked skeptical. "Oh?"

"Really, Dad." Lissy gave her father's arm a light slap. "You don't have to be all business. This is Rio! He lived with us for—well, it seems like forever, but how long was it?" She blinked.

"Till I was eighteen," Rio said.

"I forgot," said Lissy. "Your mother was with us even before you were born. I remember hanging out in the kitchen while she was cooking. You were just a baby and she kept you in a basket, right beside the potatoes and onions. I thought she might chop you up, but then I couldn't have been more than four." She laughed as if this was a delightful story.

Not even Meg dared to check out how Rio was taking that cozy memory. Was Lissy oblivious? Did she actually not know how the Stones' housekeeper had come to be a single mother?

"And I was so happy to find out that Mrs. Carefoot is still here," Lissy continued. "It wouldn't be the ranch without her."

"Where have you been living?" Rio asked.

"Oh, here and there," his half sister said. "I went to Paris after school but soon found out that classroom French isn't like the real thing. Then I tried marriage—to a Parisian—but that didn't work out except for improving my language skills, so I came back home. I'm thinking of making myself useful. I could be a French teacher if all else fails." She stopped. "Not that there's a big call for that in Wyoming. But we won't be here much longer, I suppose." She stopped again. The glance she threw her father was laced with expectation. "When Dad said you were back, I persuaded him that we had to pay you a visit."

Rio scrubbed his hands on the tail of his shirt. His work boots were caked with chaff-flecked manure. Uneasily, he scraped his soles against the pebbled ground. "Then this is a social call."

"Of a sort," Stone said.

"You can take them up to the house," Meg said. She didn't suppose Rio wanted to entertain in the one-room bunkhouse, especially the Stones. Their closets were probably larger. With better lighting, lined in smooth-sanded cedar instead of ancient, crumbling logs.

Rio's eyes flicked her way. Something in the look made her say, "Follow me."

They trooped silently up to the ranch house. The original homestead had been made of logs, which were now lost under clapboard siding and multiple additions of no particular style. The best thing about the house was the wide front porch with a low wall of fieldstone. Turn the corner and the view of the river and mountains was spectacular.

The interior wouldn't impress the Stones. Meg shoved aside the tangle of outerwear to hang her jacket on a hook, wishing she'd followed through with her plan to empty out the junk. "I'll make coffee," she said, leaving Rio to settle his company in the dowdy living room.

Minutes later, the sound of raised voices reached her. She shut off the water to listen, holding the old used coffee filter in midair. Brown droplets splattered the countertop.

Rio's low voice cut through Lissy Stone's babble and her father's rumble. "How do you know about it?"

"That's not the point," said Stone.

Lissy's laugh quavered. "He has his spies."

"No one knows except—" Rio stopped midstream.

Me. Meg tossed out the soggy filter. *And his mother.*

"You have no rights over me." Rio.

Hastily Meg scooped granules and switched on the coffeemaker, then edged into the dining room for a better listening position. They had to be talking about the book.

"I have every right to protect my reputation." Stone, sounding stuffy. "And my family."

"Your family." Rio again. To Meg's ears, it was obvious that he'd barely managed to leave out the word *legitimate.*

"Honestly, Dad." Lissy was trying to mollify the unmollifiable. "Rio wouldn't expose us to public ridicule."

"Melissa," Stone snapped, "go see about the coffee."

Rats. Meg moved quickly out of the dining room and got busy with the silverware. "Coming up," she said brightly when Lissy walked into the room.

"I've been banished." Lissy sighed. "My father is so medieval about these things. All that bluster about primogeniture."

Meg searched the cupboard for matching cups. She resorted to the china cabinet. She took her time, straining to catch the rumble of male voices. They'd toned down after the first outburst. Eventually she had to return to the kitchen with an armful of her mother's china. She set the cups on a tray one by one, including the creamer, sugar dish and saucers. Never let it be said that Miss Lennox didn't have class.

Lissy was idly examining her nails, as if she didn't mind being shunted aside. As if she had nothing at stake.

"I doubt that Rio is threatening the line of ascension." The Stones might think of themselves as Wyoming royalty, but Meg wasn't bowing or scraping. Rio shouldn't have to either.

"It's really all about the family name." Lissy strolled around the kitchen, taking in the print wallpaper and the ragged dish towel hanging on the handle of the stove. "You wouldn't understand."

"Meaning?"

Lissy spun to give Meg a compensatory smile. "Your father didn't care what people thought of him."

"How did you know my father?"

"I didn't. But that's what I heard."

"From who?"

"Well, my father, I suppose. And Billy."

Meg didn't understand. She hadn't been aware of any dealings between her father and the Stones, but then a lot might have happened in the time she'd been away. "Your brother's still around?"

"He comes and goes." Lissy considered the dinged-up kitchen chair judiciously before taking a seat. She tilted her head at Meg. "You're keeping Rio all to yourself again, hmm—just like old times?"

"He's working for me."

"Until the book sells?"

"Then you do know about the book."

"That's all anyone at home talks about anymore." Lissy folded her hands in her lap. "I had no idea that Rio was a writer, but he does fit the type, doesn't he? So silent and brooding and romantic. What do you think?"

"I think I'd better keep my mouth shut."

"THIS MEMOIR," Stone said. "You'll have to put a stop to it. I refuse to let you abuse my reputation." He was direct about his demands, you had to give him that.

Rio was punchy. No wonder. Stone and his daughter had tag-teamed him. Good cop, bad cop. Some sugar from Lissy, a lot of sting from Stone.

He breathed deeply, sticking to his decision not to rub the man's nose in his own mess. For the moment. But he couldn't go without comment on Stone's hypocrisy. "So even after all this time you're still concerned about your reputation. What about my mother's?"

"Boy, you don't know what went on there."

"You took advantage of her loneliness."

"It wasn't like that."

Rio didn't care to find out what had drawn his mother to Stone. But he had gained enough maturity to allow that the benefits of the affair might not have been as one-sided as he'd once supposed. No one knew better than he that you could keep on loving someone even after incontrovertible proof that they were no good for you.

"Whatever happened, she was the one who suffered. You continued as if nothing had occurred."

Stone got huffy. "Ginny never suffered! I saw to that."

"Keeping her on salary as a housekeeper? Big of you."

"I was generous."

"She worked hard. Still does."

"I've offered her a retirement package. A generous one."

That was news. But Rio didn't want to give the man any credit. "Time to clear the decks?"

"I'm getting older."

Not dying, Rio told himself, refusing to admit the pang of regret he felt at the idea that there'd never be any kind of forgiveness or understanding between them. And that would also be his own fault, especially after the book.

Don't weaken now. Rio's gut tightened. Even though Stone had aged, he'd always been healthy as a horse. He probably believed that he was entitled to live forever.

"It's time to consider my legacy." Stone looked at Rio balefully.

He returned the stare. Wondering if the hint of inheritance was supposed to cow him into obedience.

"You see, I have an image to protect," Stone continued. "Your book could tarnish that."

Cry me a river.

"OH, MEG." Lissy giggled. "What's the harm in a bit of girl talk?"

"We've never had that kind of relationship."

"No, we were too busy battling over Rio." Lissy made owl eyes. "Little did I know that he was actually my brother."

Meg wondered who'd told her, but she wouldn't ask. Rio's business should be his own.

Lissy lowered her voice to a whisper. "I presume Rio's told you that he and I share a father."

Meg nodded with reluctance as she filled the sugar bowl. "A long time ago."

"I didn't find out until I was away at boarding school. Billy always knew, though. So he says." Lissy frowned. "I'm not sure I believe him, but if he did, I'd have liked to know sooner that I had a half brother. Things might have been different."

"How?"

"We could have been friends. All of us."

Meg doubted that. On the many occasions when the Stone siblings weren't being monitored by their appearance-conscious mother, Rio had suffered at their hands for being no more than the son of their housekeeper. They'd ordered him around as if he worked for them, too. Then suddenly, on other days, they'd been all smiles and sharing, claiming to want to be his pal. Being the poor relation wouldn't have improved his lot, either way.

After shaking several store-bought cookies onto a plate, Meg could find no more to do with the coffee tray. She lifted it. "Shall we?"

"We shall." Lissy wiggled her eyebrows. "Let's go reorder my father's priorities."

Meg almost liked her at that moment. Lissy wasn't quite the snob that she'd believed. But she still doubted they'd ever be friends. Their ideas of Rio's welfare were probably very different. Meg's instinct was to protect. Lissy seemed to want to promote.

Rio's own plans might undo them both.

SEEING HE WAS getting nowhere, Stone added, "And there's your mother to consider."

Rio frowned. The man knew where to twist the knife. "Don't worry. I'm considering her."

"And what about her?" Stone nodded toward the kitchen.

"Lissy?"

"The other one."

"Meg?"

"How does she feel about having her past exposed?"

Rio gripped the arms of the chair. "That's not your business."

Stone's eyes gleamed beneath knitted brows. "Then she's not supportive?"

"I didn't say that." Rio looked away. Wan sunlight streamed through the picture window, scarcely improving the dreariness of the room. Meg had taken down the old curtains, but had made no other changes to the room that they'd rarely occupied as children. Or now, for that matter.

A random thought struck him: The house needed life. Children.

He shook his head. "I'll take care of Meg. My mother, too."

"What does that mean?"

Both men turned. Meg and Lissy stood in the doorway to the dining room. Lissy's face was blank, but Meg's expression betrayed her. She strode over and plunked a tray on the coffee table. "I take care of myself just fine, thank you."

Did she? Rio studied her. The long hair, falling to

hide her narrow face, her pink mouth and wounded eyes. Even though they'd managed to find an uneasy peace in the past few days, she was still no more forth-coming than she had been at his arrival. He had hoped that she'd have relaxed by now.

"I know you can, Meg. I wasn't saying—"

"Please serve yourselves." She made a sharp gesture. "I have to go. I left my horse tied up."

The door banged behind her.

"Well," Lissy said brightly as she sat on the sofa and lifted the hot carafe to pour, "she certainly hasn't changed."

Rio couldn't agree. But he still didn't know why.

CHAPTER NINE

MEG EASED ONE of their lighter-weight western saddles onto the mustang's back. The mare hunched and quivered. Her hindquarters jounced up and down a couple of times, but soon she settled into an uneasy acceptance, standing tethered to a post, her ears swiveling and head turning to follow Meg's every movement.

Rio also watched. She walked around the mare, keeping close contact by sliding her hand along the horse's flanks. She spoke in a low voice that began to soothe him, too.

The Stones had gone. When Meg didn't return from the barn even then, he'd walked over to roust her, halfway thinking of demanding a few answers. But seeing her with the mustang had changed his mind.

As much as waiting wore his patience, Meg needed more time. One day, she would tell him her reasons for running away. And she would open up about what had hurt her so much while she was gone.

Slowly she dropped the stirrups. The mare flinched a little at the new weight dangling at her sides. Meg stood at the horse's head, running a hand back and forth along her neck. "See? It's not so bad. Not so bad."

"Take it slow enough and a—a horse can get used to almost anything." Rio was thinking of leaving Treetop, joining the army. The regulations and order had appealed to him, but not the lifestyle itself. He'd adjusted. He'd lived through the deprivation, the frustration, the sudden death of soldiers who were the only brothers he'd ever known. But living without Meg was becoming impossible.

She raised her eyes. "Hullo, Rio."

"Meg." He'd said her name a thousand times to himself during the years they'd been apart. Maybe a hundred thousand. She'd been his prayer in hard times, his promise during the longest nights.

Finally they were together. And yet she remained so far away.

"They gone?"

She couldn't have missed their departure, but he only nodded. "It's safe to come out of the barn."

Meg lifted the saddle slightly, then resettled it. She dropped the cinch and let it dangle. "Some surprise."

"I'd guessed this was coming, eventually."

"How come?"

"I expected that Stone would hear of the book."

"Not from me," she said defensively.

"I realize that." He'd wondered, briefly, if she'd told someone else. Queenie Briggs, perhaps. At heart he'd guessed, though. It had been his mother. She was still loyal to the Stones. Mr. Stone, first and foremost.

That was hurtful to admit, but how could Rio blame her? Stone might not have given her the love and respect she deserved, but her place at the ranch had been there even when her son wasn't.

Meg was watching him across the saddle. "You think the book is all he came for?"

"Hell, yeah."

"What about Lissy?"

"Hard to say. She was friendly. That could have been an act. Trying to get on my good side, in case her father's hardball tactics didn't work."

"Did they?"

He clenched his teeth. His mouth tasted like tinfoil. "I'm not choosing to suit him, that's for sure."

He might take the easy way out for Meg, but she'd never ask.

"What if Lissy wants to be your sister?"

Rio parked a boot heel on the bottom rail. "We'll see. I've never thought of her that way."

The summer he was sixteen, he'd been stopped for speeding in one of the ranch trucks. Sophie Ryan, the deputy, had probably seen the frantic scramble in the front seat as he and Meg switched places, but she'd chosen to let them off with only a word of warning for their parents. Meg's father and his mother had come to a quick agreement that their offsprings' friendship had become too volatile. They would be separated for the summer.

Meg, still fifteen, had been grounded. Rio had been sent to live for a few months with his mother's family on the Crow reservation near Billings. There, he'd been welcomed with open arms. He'd experienced the kind of close family life he'd never had at the ranch. But he'd been homesick. Lovesick, too.

After noticing how frequently talk had hushed whenever he walked into a room, he'd kept his ear to the ground. Eventually he'd overheard his grandmother on the phone giving a progress report to his mother. She'd scolded her daughter for keeping Rio's father's identity a secret, particularly when the two of them were living under the same roof.

Under the same roof. Rio's face had burned with humiliation as he realized what that meant.

William Walker Stone was his father.

And the man had lived his life as if Rio was nothing. Not even worthy of notice.

Rio had come home in September, intending to confront his mother. Maybe even Stone. But she'd been ill while he was away, ending up in the hospital for a gall-bladder operation. He'd locked away his anger, and only told Meg about the secret after swearing her to secrecy. As far as he'd been aware, she had never broken the promise not to tell.

"Lissy never told me she's aware who my father is," he said.

Neither had Stone. Other than giving him the base-ball glove, the only time the man had shown any interest in Rio was after he'd been arrested. Virginia had begged Stone to use his influence to keep their son's record clean. He'd done that much, but the only acknowl-edgment that Rio had received for agreeing to the deal was a lecture about sacrificing himself for the good of his country. Stone was a gung-ho, rally-for-the-stars-and-stripes type of politician, although of course Billy had never enlisted.

"Oh, Lissy knows," Meg said. "She told me so, in the kitchen."

"What did she say?"

"Called him medieval. There was something about protecting the family name. But I think she was sincere about wanting you as a brother." While she spoke, Meg had loosely clasped the cinch, then released it. She put up the stirrups and removed the saddle. The mustang's ears were pricked, but she remained remarkably calm. Rio suspected that somewhere in her murky past, she'd been worked with before.

Meg walked over and placed the saddle over the rail near Rio. "Would you like that, finally getting a sister?"

"It would be strange."

"And there's Billy, too. Lissy said he's always known."

"I doubt it. He wouldn't have kept such a juicy secret to himself when he could have taunted me with it."

"Maybe he's changed."

Rio shook his head. "People don't change that much."

Meg frowned, carving the line between her eyes deeper. "I hope they can."

He reached through the rails to her. She resisted for a moment, then let him squeeze her hand. "I didn't mean you."

She lifted a shoulder, trying to shrug him off.

"What changed you, Meg?" he asked gently.

"Who says anything has?" she asked scornfully, sounding like her father.

"Then what do you want to change?"

She pulled away, as he'd expected. She returned to Axxaashe and removed the saddle blanket and the halter. The mustang trotted away, her cream tail swishing across her hocks as she greeted her colt, removed for the training session to the adjacent corral.

Meg climbed onto the bottom rail and slung one leg across the fence. She perched there, watching the mustang with a fond smile. "Five bucks says she rolls."

Rio nodded agreement, even though it was a sucker bet. The mare's knees were already buckling. She circled, almost went down, then circled again before dropping with a soft grunt. The sand wasn't soft enough for a really good roll, but she made do, twisting her body with all four legs up in the air.

Meg laughed, her eyes glinting as she nudged Rio's shoulder. "Pay up."

"Nope. That one makes us even."

She laughed again as the mare lurched to her feet and shook off a cloud of dust. "I forgot."

He took a chance and wrapped his hands around her waist to swing her to the ground. She was almost as slim as she'd been as a girl, and for a moment made sharp with memory he held her aloft at arm's length before putting her down.

She staggered slightly. He used the momentum to pull her toward him. "Five bucks says you won't let me kiss you."

"I won't," she said emphatically, before realizing the quandary. "But if I don't, I lose the bet."

"That's the catch." He lowered his chin. "How much do you want that five dollars?"

She flushed, yanking herself away. "Not that much."

He caught her from behind with an arm around the waist and bent his cheek to hers. She was silk and suede and spice. He was hoarse; he could scarcely get words out. "Why do you always run from me?"

"Because—" She turned her face but she couldn't get away. "Because you want too much." She caught her breath as he squeezed her tighter. "You always have."

"I wanted you to love me."

She struggled, turning and pushing at him. "I did!"

He released her. "But not enough."

"I was only sixteen the first time we…did it. Barely eighteen the night I ran away." She backed away slowly, her eyes huge. "It was too soon to make any kind of lasting commitment."

He held his palms open to her. "Not for me."

She froze, her only movement a visible swallow.

Axxaashe trotted around the paddock, head held high. Her hooves made the ground vibrate. "Why are you doing this now? Didn't your father cause enough turmoil?"

Rio was vibrating from the inside, too. "Maybe that's why. We need to get things out in the open instead of avoiding the obvious. Always looking the other way instead of at each other."

"This was supposed to be a professional relationship."

"That was never happening."

"What about your book? Doesn't that come first?" She pulled her head back. Tilted her chin as her eyebrows came together. "Or is this for the book?"

He scoffed. "Come on."

"Maybe you need a—a—" One hand waved. "A better ending."

A happy ending. He longed for that, but had few expectations of actually achieving one with Meg.

"Or drama," she snapped. "More drama. I may have provided it in the past, but I'm done with that." She wheeled. "I want to be left alone."

He strode after her. "If you really did, you wouldn't have hired me."

She halted abruptly, then turned on him, raising a fist to thump on his chest. "I felt sorry for you."

He covered her fist with his hand, dropped it to belt level. She was so close he could feel the charged ions bouncing in the narrow space between them. "Pity, Meg? I don't think so."

Her only answer was a sharp inhale.

"You've been wanting this." His voice was guttural with his own stark need as he took her in his arms and lowered his mouth to hers. He'd been dreaming of kissing Meg again for far too long. His longing turned the embrace into a wild, clutching thing.

Meg was the first to pull away, although her hands remained resting against his hip bones. "I realize I owe you a lot." He heard the regret in her voice. "But we can't go back to the way we used to be."

The October wind rose to a moan. The old barn creaked. A few remaining dead leaves broke free of the bare branches to join the swirl of debris along the edges of the driveway.

Rio cradled Meg's head against his chest. He'd faced gunfire and grenades, but he didn't have the courage to look into her eyes just then.

"We can go forward." But even to him, the words seemed hollow. There could be no future with Meg until they'd redeemed their past.

THE MAILBOX AT THE END of the driveway was a mangled mess, hanging off the top of the tilted post by one bolt. Rio gave the log post a shove with his boot and the whole thing toppled over with the sound of cracking wood.

"It was rotten anyway," he said. "I'll drive into town and get a new box, then replace the whole shebang before the mail arrives this afternoon."

Meg knelt and wrenched open the creased door, trying to remember when she'd last picked up the mail. She felt inside the box, as crumpled as a beer can, but it was empty.

She glanced up at Rio. "Did you hear anything last night?"

"Nope. You?"

"I was dead to the world." Around midnight, she'd taken a Sominex, something she'd avoided since beginning her health kick. Rio had awakened her not fifteen minutes ago by pounding on her bedroom door, calling her outside to see the destruction that had happened during the night.

Her scalp prickled. "Mailbox baseball is not unusual." But the metal box had taken more than one swing of a bat from a moving vehicle. It had been deliberately smashed beyond use.

"Uh-huh." Rio was looking at the tire tracks. They veered off the blacktop, gouged into the hard-packed dirt. "Let's walk up to the Vaughns'."

Rising, Meg eyed him suspiciously. "What for?"

"See if they've still got a mailbox. If it was kids out joyriding, they don't usually stop at one."

Meg followed him, even though she didn't really want to go. She just couldn't think of an excuse. She also didn't want him to see how reluctant she truly was.

He slowed to let her catch up, then put his hand between her shoulder blades as they trudged along the roadway.

A friendly gesture, she told herself. Reassuring.

He knows. Even when they were just little kids, he'd been the one to see beneath her bravado to the girl who'd wanted approval most of all.

Meg walked on. Rio's hand remained, magically manufacturing warmth in her bones through her layers of suede and sheepskin, flannel and a thick wool undershirt. Weeks ago, even days ago, she'd have bolted from the display of intimacy.

Had she changed? Or simply become more accustomed to having him around?

Or had the kiss transformed her?

"Don't count on it," she muttered.

"What was that?"

She shoved her hands into the deep pockets of her jacket. "Nothing. Talking to myself."

He stopped. "Look there."

The sun was up, drawing a pale gold scrim across the pasture bordering the road. Three deer grazed among a stand of saplings, their autumn coats a rich reddish-brown.

Pebbles crunched under Meg's heel. One of the deers' heads came up and an instant later they'd bounded away into the trees, flashing their haunches and the white flags of their upright tails.

"Nice and healthy looking," Meg said.

"You craving venison for the winter?"

"Uh-uh. Are you planning to hunt?"

"I'm not keen on it."

"Do you have a firearm, from the army?"

"No."

"Not even as a keepsake?"

He made a dismissive sound and she felt stupidly blundering as she remembered the short passage she'd read that day in the bunkhouse. "Sorry. I'm not sure how to, um, talk to you about the war. You seem well adjusted, considering."

"I'm okay. One of the lucky ones."

Ten minutes later, they were approaching the neighboring ranch. A tall signpost bearing the Double V brand arched over the driveway. Meg slowed. "Box's intact. We can go back."

Rio touched her arm. His head tilted encouragingly. "Come on."

She met his eyes. In the morning light, they were brighter than usual, shimmering in the dark, cool depths. "You're so transparent."

"I didn't bust up the mailbox."

The Vaughns' house was a shingled two-story, closer to the road than her place. Ellis Vaughn came around the corner, saw them and waved. Rio waved back, propelling Meg forward with his arm around her waist.

She gave up resisting as they crossed beneath the arch. The Vaughns had been good to her. It was shameful that she hadn't made at least a courtesy call before now. "Hello, Mr. Vaughn," she hailed. "Remember me?"

Though he had to be close to seventy-five, there was nothing wrong with his memory. "Good to see you,

Margaret Jo." That had been Meg's mother's way of introducing her as a child. The older generation, those who knew her back when, often used the name. "The wife's been hoping you'd call."

"I've meant to," Meg mumbled.

Carmen Vaughn was already opening the front door, a woman settled comfortably in her late sixties, wearing an apron tied over a zippered tracksuit. "Saw you coming up the drive as I was finishing the breakfast dishes." Her expression was serious as she considered Meg, but kind. "Come in for coffee," she invited, after they'd finished the hellos all around. "I can offer fresh cinnamon rolls."

"We had some trouble at Wild River," Rio started, after they were settled at the kitchen table. He explained about the busted mailbox and the stone-throwing incident. "You've had no trouble up this way?"

"Nothin' I've noticed." Mr. Vaughn rubbed a finger beneath his silver scrub-brush mustache. "But I don't get about as well as I used to."

His wife patted his knobby-knuckled hand. "You do fine."

Meg's attention had strayed from the cheerful yellow walls and poppy-print curtains to the window that overlooked the western side of the property, where the outbuildings were situated. The old barn had been set back the farthest, used only for hay storage before it had burned. From the house, the roof had been just visible over the rise of the hay field.

She scanned the brown stubble. They hadn't rebuilt.

"You've noticed our new babies," Mrs. Vaughn said, following Meg's glance. She got up and approached a large carton sitting beneath the window. Only then did Meg hear the soft whimpers and scrabble of toenails against cardboard.

Mrs. Vaughn reached into the carton and came out with a squirming handful of gray fuzz. "Eight weeks old. Our Gracie's last litter. We're having her fixed."

Mr. Vaughn chuckled. "That's what you said last time."

"Puppies," Rio said with delight. He grinned at Meg. "I swear—I had no idea."

Mrs. Vaughn placed the small creature in Meg's lap. The puppy was a speckled gray with dark floppy ears and a short tail tipped in white. "Do you remember Gracie? She was only a pup herself the last time you were home. This is her third litter. The male you're holding is the pick of the bunch. A real scrapper."

"Cute," Meg said. The puppy squirmed so eagerly she could hardly hold on. She had to cradle it against her front. The animal rooted at her collar, licking with a warm wet tongue until she giggled.

"Meg's been wanting a dog," said Rio.

She shot him a glare, but she couldn't hold it. Her chin was being tickled by puppy whiskers and a wiggly puppy nose.

Mr. Vaughn crossed his hands over his chest. "Then there you go."

His wife was equally satisfied. "I'll earmark him for you. They'll be ready to adopt in a week or two."

"Not now?" Rio said. Probably afraid that Meg would back out, given an opportunity.

"I guess I'm fussy," Mrs. Vaughn said. "I just like to keep them with their mother as long as possible. Or maybe it's with me!" She laughed. "But if the pup's going to a good home, maybe…"

"Oh, no, I'm not taking him." Meg thrust the animal at Rio. "He's all yours."

"Sure, I'll take one as soon as they're ready." The puppy tried to climb onto Rio's shoulder. Under the window, the box bulged, barely containing the wriggling mass of the rest of the litter. The mother, a small mixed-breed terrier, was looking over the top, her ears perked in the direction of the missing pup.

Meg gave the box a dubious glance. "How many?"

"Just four this time." Mr. Vaughn chuckled. "They're not purebreds, but they've got lots of terrier in 'em. Good ranch dogs."

"We don't have any stock to round up," Meg said lightly. "Just a few horses."

"So's I heard. You're boarding?"

"And training."

"She's working with a mustang now." The puppy was gnawing on Rio's finger. He looked up at Meg, sending her a signal she didn't get. "But there's a bit of a problem with the colt. Needs to be weaned and we don't have the space."

"Bring him over here," Mr. Vaughn said. "Our barn's practically empty. We've cut down to the bare minimum stock, just our chickens and the one old milk cow Carmen won't let me sell."

"Old Betsy Blue's been with us longer than some of our kids."

"That's a generous offer," Meg said without accepting.

Rio had no such reservation. "I'll lead him over this afternoon, if that's okay." Normally, they'd have kept the foal at home to watch him closely, but Meg needed to work with the dam.

"That'll give me time to fix up a stall," Mr. Vaughn said.

"Don't go to any trouble on my account." Meg felt almost desperate.

"No trouble. It'll be nice to have some extra company around the place." Mr. Vaughn grinned at his wife. "Maybe weaning the foal will save us from acquiring another litter or flock. Carmen does likes her babies."

Too much baby talk for Meg. She shifted in her chair while the two men discussed logistics and feeding times.

Absently Rio played with the puppy. It nibbled at his fingers, looking far too adorable in the coat of salt-and-pepper fuzz. There was a white patch on its chest, where the fur met in a swirl.

She looked down. Her hands were clenched in her lap. "I, um, see that you never rebuilt the old barn."

Mr. Vaughn broke off his conversation with Rio. "We didn't really need it anymore. Even then, our herd was small. We were selling most of our hay."

"You see," Mrs. Vaughn said kindly to Rio, "it was no great loss."

Her husband chuckled. "The insurance money came in handy."

Meg and Rio exchanged a look. "Still." She cleared her throat. "I owe you an apology. I'm sorry that it's coming so late."

Mrs. Vaughn was confused. "You…?"

Meg took a breath. "It was me—I was to blame. I started the fire. Not Rio."

The kitchen went silent. Even the puppies seemed to be listening. Meg couldn't continue.

"Well." Mrs. Vaughn was flustered. "My goodness."

Meg found her grit. "I was trespassing. The barn was just somewhere to hang out for a couple of hours until—well, that doesn't matter. Rio was there, for a while." She glanced at him and he nodded, giving her the courage to continue. "I was smoking. I'm not sure what happened. I must have been careless. Someone came to pick me up and—" She shrugged. "I didn't notice anything wrong when we left, but I have to assume I left a butt smoldering."

Mrs. Vaughn frowned. "But why did Rio confess?"

"I'd taken off," Meg said miserably. "I didn't even know about the fire, or that Rio was under suspicion. I didn't know anything."

"I reported Rio," Mr. Vaughn said. "I was closing up for the night and I saw him leaving the old hay barn. You kids were all over the countryside, so I didn't think much of it until we woke up to the fire."

Meg bowed her head. "It wasn't Rio. It was me."

Mr. Vaughn scowled. "Then I don't understand why you'd admit to starting the fire, son."

Rio finally spoke. "I didn't want them going after Meg."

"But, Rio!" she blurted. "I was gone. I didn't make contact with anyone in Treetop for months. They might not have found me, even if they'd been looking."

"What about Kris's family?" he said. "The Addamos knew you'd run off with him. And he came back, just a week later."

"We had a falling-out," she mumbled. A nice way of putting it. She'd realized within their first day on the road that she'd made a mistake, choosing Kris as her partner in crime. She'd already missed Rio. But she'd been too stubborn to go back.

That night, when Rio had come to find her in the Vaughns' barn, it hadn't been for a last-ditch reconciliation or a sentimental goodbye. Instead, he'd bluntly told her that rather than running away, she should stay to make amends with her father. She should just grow up already.

That had angered her—an anger that had fired her departure but sputtered out all too soon. Even so, growing up enough to return had taken her ten years.

Mrs. Vaughn clucked her tongue. "What a shame for Rio."

Meg was shriveled inside, but she wouldn't let herself make excuses. "I've felt bad about the whole thing for a long time. I wish I'd returned when I first learned what had happened, but Rio was already enlisted. There didn't seem to be anything to gain." She looked at her neighbors. "Except of course that I still owed you an apology. And repayment."

"We'll take the apology sure enough," said Mr. Vaughn gruffly, "though there's nothing to repay."

"That old barn was practically falling down." Mrs. Vaughn got up to rescue a puppy who'd managed to wriggle onto the edge of the cardboard box. The nursing mother dog whined. "Don't fuss, Miss Gracie. You'll get her back soon enough."

She returned to the table, holding the puppy up to her face and making kissing noises. "This is the only female of the bunch. A harum-scarum little girl. She bosses all her brothers." She made a motion toward Meg with the puppy, a match to the one in Rio's arms except for the dark circles that ringed both eyes like a pair of oversize shades.

Meg was too relieved to object to taking the little female. She couldn't quite believe that the confession she'd dreaded was over so simply. The Vaughns seemed satisfied, and when Meg looked at Rio, he was smiling at her.

The puppy nuzzled her ear, her nose damp. Hot tears

gathered at the corners of Meg's eyes. With a deep sigh, she lowered her face to the soft gray fur and let herself be, for once, comforted.

CHAPTER TEN

THE WHINNIES COMING from the paddock were sometimes shrill and desperate, sometimes low and searching. The mustang mare had been calling for her colt off and on all afternoon, into the evening. The sound of it was shredding Meg's heart. The silences between the entreaties were almost as bad.

She flung the pillow aside and climbed out of bed. Rio had taken Whirligig to the Double V to be weaned, a wrenching experience for both horses. For Meg, too, even though she'd put on a tough front, continuing with her work as normal.

The mare had still been restless when Rio had returned. She'd paced the fence, shown no interest in her evening grain or the hay net. Meg had worried out loud, but Rio had reassured her that the separation anxiety wouldn't last past a few days. Some mares gave almost no trouble at all.

Even a few days of this was too long for Meg to bear.

She felt around in the dark for her jeans and slipped them on. Rio had stayed up at the house after dinner, a transparent effort to distract her. They'd watched a DVD, but she couldn't even remember the title.

The corrals had gone temporarily silent. When Meg crossed beneath the light outside the barn door, the mare roused herself with an eager nicker. Her nose thrust between the railings, nostrils whiffling.

"I'm sorry, Axxaashe." Meg stroked the velvet muzzle. "It's only me."

She whispered comfort to the mare, but there was little to be had. The mustang swung away, turning restlessly in the confined space of the narrow corral, every now and then giving a soft whickering plea to the cold night air.

Meg closed her eyes, listening, almost believing she could hear Gig's answering peal although he was shut up far away in the Vaughns' barn. The mare's ears flickered.

"It'll get easier," Meg whispered to the mustang. Her fingers curled around the railings. "You'll see. Tomorrow, or the next day…you won't miss him so much."

Suddenly she turned. A dark form stood silhouetted by the barn light.

For a fleeting second Meg thought it might be her vandal, but then the man moved closer and she saw he was Rio, gravely handsome, his hands outstretched.

She went to him. His name soft on her tongue. "Rio."

He sighed. "Meg."

"You came for the mare."

"If that's what you want to—"

"You didn't?"

There was a moment of silence before he confessed in low, thick tones, "I came for you." His arms went around her. "I knew you'd be here."

She pressed against him. "I—I couldn't stand it anymore."

"She's quiet now."

"But so alone."

"Not really. The other horses will keep her company."

Meg's head wagged. Her fingers clenched on the fleece wadding of his pullover. "It's not the same."

"No, but she'll survive."

The ache in Meg's throat had become a raw wound. "Probably. I did."

Rio's head came up. His body was taut. "What are you saying? You…?"

"No. Oh, no." She was stricken, knowing that she had to lie, or at least evade. "I meant losing, or, or leaving someone you love."

His hands were a vise on her elbows as he set her back a little. "Your father? Your mother?"

She nodded. "And you."

"Aw, Meggie." Again, he clasped her to his chest. She felt his heartbeat, like a distant drum, a steady, stirring cadence.

He was stroking her now, his fingers at her nape, sinking into her hair, touching beneath her chin to lift her mouth. The first gentle kiss rapidly became a seeking embrace, driven by too many weeks of pent-up passion.

Meg's resistance was so low it was nonexistent. She'd needed him for such a long time that it seemed like forever. Her resolution to remain solo and self-reliant didn't seem very important with Rio's arms around her and his lips on hers, offering reassurance.

A respite.

And release.

Arm in arm, they walked up to the house. Not speaking. The silent accord felt like old times to Rio, back when they were young but not entirely innocent, before Meg had been lured away by other boys. He'd naively thought that they would always be that way, fifteen and sixteen, on the cusp of what had seemed like maturity at the time.

But he'd been too serious, and she'd been too un-tamed.

"I was proud of you today," he said, "at the Vaughns'."

"Don't be." She slid out of her jacket. "It was too little, too late."

"Give yourself some credit. That took guts, standing up and admitting what'd happened."

"What happened," she echoed. "Right. I wish I knew for sure."

"Wish I knew at all."

Her gaze slipped sidelong, an evasive maneuver he recognized by now.

"The fight with your father…"

"That was nothing new," she said, but her voice was clipped.

She and her father had battled over almost everything she did, but Rio was certain that on the night she'd run away there'd been some specific reason. He'd never forgotten the look on Meg's face as she'd huddled in the dilapidated barn, hugging herself, giving him monotone one-syllable responses. Gnawing her nails. Shaking her head. Refusing his attempts to get her to make amends with her dad, or at least some overture toward understanding.

She'd been beyond his help. He'd gone away convinced something inside her was broken. To this day, he couldn't say that she'd healed.

"He never hurt you?"

Meg kicked off her boots. "Physically? No, of course not. We were just always at odds." She sighed. "Over everything."

"He wanted better for you. He just wasn't good at expressing that." Her dad's every word had come out harsh. Every comment a criticism.

"Maybe."

"Sure, he was rough on you, but allow the man some leeway. He was as bewildered as you." Rio ran his knuckles along her cheek. She bit her bottom lip. "You were too much for the guy. He didn't get that what you needed was unconditional approval. You wanted to feel secure."

"Aren't you smart."

Rio looped his arms around her. "Am I wrong?"

"No," she admitted, leaning her head against his shoulder. "Too bad I wouldn't listen to you then, either."

"Will you now?"

"I'm giving it a shot."

"Honestly? I'd rather listen to you. Talk to me, Meg. Trust me."

She made a gulping sound that started out as a laugh. "Jeez, Rio. I haven't changed that much. I'd still rather screw than talk."

"Aw, Meggie."

Her eyes narrowed. "Do you think taking me to bed will make everything all right again? Because it won't. It'll only be sex." She pushed away from him. "Not part of our original arrangement, no. But still only sex."

He wasn't put off. That was Meg—blunt and direct. Didn't matter. There was more inside her. The Meg she was afraid to be.

All he said was, "You're so wrong," while taking her by the hand and leading her through the hallway. The bedroom was dark, but he could see the faded floral wallpaper and the pine four-poster with rumpled bedclothes. Meg's old things were jammed into a corner cupboard with open shelves—a floppy stuffed animal, her rock collection, a pair of spurs with cracked leather and tarnished buckles, the beat-up straw cowboy hat she used to wear every summer. The copy of *Catcher in the Rye* he'd given her on her fifteenth birthday, thinking he was being deep and meaningful. Leftovers from childhood.

She was suddenly nervous. "I don't know about this."

"It's just me, Meg."

"You're different." She watched with wide eyes as he lifted his top shirt over his head. His hair crackled with electricity. "I'm different."

"I should hope so." He removed his long-sleeved undershirt.

She stared, her eyes pinpoints of light that traced heat across his chest. "Rio?"

"Yes."

Her smile was flirty, but her hands trembled as she un-buttoned her pajama top. "That's what I was going to say."

"Yes? You were going to say yes?"

"Oh, yes."

The slight inner curves of her bare breasts came into view. The hollow of her rib cage. He wanted to touch her more than he wanted to take his next breath, but he couldn't seem to move.

She shimmied out of her jeans, plucked a drawstring and dropped her flannel bottoms. Except for the open top and a pair of thick wool socks wadded up around her ankles, she was nude. Slim and pale, graceful as a doe, perhaps even as shy, her hair hanging loose around her shoulders and her eyes filled with stars.

The Meg of his fantasies, sharp edges blurred by the unknown years that stood between them.

Talking now, trying to regain the intimacy they'd lost, would only ruin the moment. He managed a halting step, then another, and suddenly she was in his arms. They were sinking onto the bed. She moved beneath him, lithe and strong. Her mouth was soft and wet, their kisses liquid. Her hands tugged at his fly.

He had imagined taking his time with her. That was impossible. The old desire, their urgent adolescent need, had returned in full force.

She had freed him. His arousal was demanding. He yanked his mouth away from hers. "I don't have a condom."

She still knew how to stroke him into hot, shocking desperation. "'Sokay," she whispered. "I'm clean. It's safe."

"What about birth con—"

"No worries." Her eyes were dark. She didn't blink.

It was easy to believe her even without details. Especially when something primal inside him wanted to give her a baby.

He scooped her breast to his mouth. She arched, meeting him, her flat belly pressing against his hip bones. The warm center of her drew him in. He filled her, giving her a moment to adjust before driving deeper as she opened for him, encouraging him with sensuous sounds. Her eyes closed in concentration.

"Sweet Meggie Jo," he whispered against her neck. *"Bia."*

She hesitated before answering, "River." The English version of his name she'd used rarely. Only when they were together like this.

He believed, because he wanted to, that meant everything was going to be okay. Not right, not even settled, but surely her using the name was a promise for the future.

MEG KNEW she'd made a mistake. Not the sex itself. There was great comfort in the way that Rio held her afterward, just being there with her. The contact was sensual and fulfilling. She could admit that.

The mistake was in letting him think she couldn't get knocked up. Because becoming pregnant wasn't really her worst problem.

Staying that way was.

She calculated the dates in her head. The likelihood of conceiving right now was minimal, even if she'd been especially fertile, which she wasn't. With a little luck, she wouldn't have to say anything to him at all.

Why did that reassurance leave her feeling so cold?

She fidgeted beneath the blanket, lying on her side and pulling the flannel sheet to her chin. Rio slung his arm around her, holding her tucked against his body. He was warm and solid. She wrapped her arms around the pillow, closed her eyes and waited for sleep.

And listened. Straining.

"She's fine," Rio said, his voice soft and warm. "She's settled down."

"Uh-huh."

"You, too." He reached up and captured one of her hands, held it loosely against her chest.

His thumb stroked her idly. Her palm. Her wrist.

Meg's eyes flew open.

She knew the instant he became aware of what he was feeling. His body tightened, jarred by the short, fast shudder that went through him.

He said, "Meg," with such tenderness she had to swallow hard to keep away the emotion. "Meg, what's this?"

Her lips were numb. "An old scar."

"On the inside of your wrist." He released that hand but dived beneath the pillow for the other. His fingers traced the matching scar, hidden by the tattoos she'd had inked around her wrists, but exposed here in the dark, under his touch.

His breathing became measured.

She waited. The hair rose on the back of her neck.

"Tell me about it," he finally said.

"Do I have to?" She manufactured a rusty laugh. Wanting like crazy to brush away her past with a pithy adage.

Like, shit happens.

Or what doesn't kill you makes you stronger.

Such a crock. In her experience, what doesn't kill you hurts a helluva lot.

"A while back, I hit bottom," she said, surprised that she was able to sound so even keeled. Being in the dark helped. Not having to look at the pity in Rio's eyes.

"I'd lost my job with the city over a load of crap that was pretty much a setup so I couldn't sue for sexual harassment. Not that I could've afforded a lawyer anyway."

She punched the pillow once before folding her fists beneath her chin. "I was drinking and smoking too much. My life seemed like a total waste, so one night after a couple of bottles of wine in the neighborhood bar, I stood up and told my friends that I might as well finish the job and waste myself for good. They thought I was joking."

Beneath the quilt, Rio's hand skimmed her hip. "But you weren't."

"Nope. I walked home and took out a razor. One of those throwaway ones that cost about a quarter. The thing did a lousy job, or maybe I was too drunk to do it right. The blood clotted before the paramedics got there. One of my friends had decided to check on me. When I didn't answer the door, she called 911."

He kissed the back of her head. "Then what?"

She was glad he was keeping cool. She couldn't have withstood his pity when she was still shamed by what she'd done. "They could have bandaged me and I'd have been fine. But one of the EMTs, his name was Jase Camillo, explained that he had to report me as a, uh, suicide attempt." She cleared her throat after forcing out the hated phrase. It seemed so weak and pathetic—*like your mother,* whispered her father's voice—when she'd prided herself on her strength. "So I ended up in counseling."

"Did that help?"

"Yeah, after I stopped resisting. Eventually I gave up drinking and drugs. Straightened out my life. Jase had started visiting me at the clinic, and before too long we'd moved in with each other. He was a good influence."

Rio raised up on one elbow and looked down at her. "Did you love him?"

"Yes."

She didn't want to admit that, either, but she had to. How else was she going to face up to—and live down—the past?

Rio's face moved closer. She felt the ends of his hair brush her cheek. "Still?" he asked heavily.

"No. After a few years, I thought things were getting serious, that we might even—" She cut off that confession. Too much to admit that once again she'd been unloved. Unlovable. "But we broke up."

"How long ago?"

"Maybe three or four months before I came here."

Gently Rio laid his hand below her navel. "Is this a rebound situation?"

She flipped around, not wanting him to touch her there. Especially when she couldn't be absolutely positive that her momentary, weak-minded mistake wouldn't turn into a major complication.

But if I was pregnant, maybe this time…

She pushed the thought away, only to be assailed by another. At least she knew that Rio would stand by her.

And maybe that was why she'd allowed the "mistake."

Wowza. Big revelation, Meggie Jo.

"I'm not pining for Jase," she said after a while, lifting her face a quarter-inch off the pillow, "if that's what you're thinking."

Rio settled back down. "Good to know." He took her hand again, holding it palm down against his chest. He ran his thumb back and forth along the scar. "Why the tattoos?"

"Shame," she muttered.

"A ring of flame," she'd told the tattoo artist. Then she'd thought of Rio. The hope, so small that she hadn't dared admit it out loud, that someday they would find their way back to each other. "And a circle of rain."

"Fire and rain," he mused. "Meg, you shouldn't be ashamed. You should be proud of yourself for going through hell and coming out the other side."

The emotion she'd battled back so many times wouldn't go away. It was filling her, lifting her. She spread her fingers against Rio's smooth skin, wanting to sink them deeper, find the handhold that would help pull her out of the dark. "I don't have much pride left."

"That's why you came home?"

"Because I was beat down?" She sighed. "Yeah."

She could feel Rio thinking, dammit. After a while he asked, "You've considered the reasons behind all of this, right?"

She dragged out an answer. "Sure. Of course. The usual suspects." Better to be glib. "My mother was dying to leave me. My father was emotionally absent. I wanted out so bad that I was even willing to hurt you, the one person—" She stopped, swallowing convulsively.

She had to say something. An apology. An appeal. But she didn't know how to beg.

"Shh, no. Listen. Don't worry." He rested his chin against the top of her head. "You'll figure it out."

But I need your help, she wanted to cry, thinking of how she'd only just picked herself up. How shaky she still was, inside. The ignominy she would suffer once his book was published.

That's right, Meggie Jo. Keep thinking of yourself first.

She touched her lips to his biceps. "Don't you worry. I will figure it out."

Perhaps she had more pride left than she'd believed. Too much, anyway, to ask him to sacrifice his second chance at success.

CHAPTER ELEVEN

FOR THE NEXT WEEK, Meg worked with the mustang every day. Perhaps it was because Axxaashe had lost her colt, but there seemed to be a growing bond between Meg and the horse. Trust. One afternoon Meg was returning from town and the mare had trotted to the fence, whickering a greeting. She'd smiled all day over that.

The Arab horse arrived, accompanied by her pretty, young owner, who took one look at Rio and declared that she'd be back for regular horseback rides. Meg figured that would last till the weather got really cold, but she'd managed to keep the opinion to herself.

The ranch became busier, and Meg worked hard. Rio required little direction. He saw what needed doing and he did it, while continuing to disappear every evening to the bunkhouse. She didn't ask how his writing was going, and he volunteered nothing. If he was bothered that she hadn't invited him back into her bed after their one night together, he didn't show it.

Meg tried not to let the distance between them bother her. She'd been the one who'd claimed, the morning after, that one night together didn't mean they were involved. But she hadn't said she never wanted him to touch her again, either.

She assumed he was intentionally giving her space.

Which was great. Just great. She had all the space she needed, but, unfortunately, far more than she really wanted. She just wasn't going to admit that out loud.

The last week of October had arrived before he finally approached her. She was grooming Axxaashe after a training session where she'd progressed to sitting astride the mare, even riding her on a tense but uneventful walk and trot around the corral. Soon enough, the mustang would be ready for a real ride, sans fences.

Meg swept the dandy brush across the mare's sleek dappled side. "No fences, *bia*. Nothing but freedom. What d'ya think of that?"

"I'd say your idea of freedom and hers are two different things," Rio said softly. *"Bia."*

Meg looked up, her face hot. So Rio was back from his daily visit to the Vaughns' place, the Double V. Looking lethally handsome and faintly amused beneath the gray felt brim of his cowboy hat.

"You'd better watch out," she said, prompted by a spurt of contrariness. "Sneaking up on a horse like that might get you kicked."

He wrapped his arms around her from behind. "What about sneaking up on a woman?"

She swung an ineffective boot, lightly thwapping the side of his leg.

He laughed and released her. Wishing that she'd

been more cooperative—her backside was tingling from the brief contact—she dropped the brush into the grooming kit and bent to retrieve a mane and tail comb.

Rio's eyes were on her. The warmth in her face slid lower.

"How was Gig?" she asked with complete nonchalance.

"Thriving. Mr. and Mrs. Vaughn have made him their pet. He might not want to come home."

"They're doing well?" She knew that Rio had begun to help the couple with some of their heavier chores.

"Yep. Pretty well set for winter. Mrs. V. asked about you. She's wondering when you'll go over for supper."

Meg shrugged. The Vaughns had issued an open invitation that she'd managed to evade so far.

"I said you were busy with the horses." Rio put a hand on Axxaashe's hindquarters, watching Meg comb the mare's long, silky mane. There were no more tangles, but she continued running the comb anyway, as if a hundred strokes were necessary.

"And a visitor," he added.

Meg froze, several long silver strands caught in the comb. "What?"

"My mother's stopping by. Any minute now, in fact."

"Why didn't you say so?"

"I just did."

"I'm a mess. I smell like horse." Meg tore the blue bandanna out of her hair, reached into a water bucket and used the bandanna to scrub her hands. "And the house." Mrs. Carefoot upheld high standards at the Stone ranch. But of course, she had plenty of hired help.

"There's a smudge on your chin." Rio took the bandanna. "Let me."

He used his fingertips to tilt up her jaw. Meg went still, her eyes narrowed. "Why's she coming?"

He dabbed. "Why not? I'm her son. It's just a normal visit."

"Nothing to do with the book?"

His expression became grim. "She's already aired her opinion on that. She thinks I should write fiction."

Meg pulled away. "That would be the easier route to take."

"Maybe you two can unite forces." Rio looked down, folding the bandanna into a neat square. "Marshal an attack."

"I wouldn't do that."

"No." He took a step toward her, but only to tuck the bandanna into her jacket pocket. "You have other means of persuasion."

He turned and walked away.

Meg's mouth hung open. She shut it, then hurriedly released the mustang into the corral. She had to run to catch up to Rio. Her outrage spilled before she'd reached him. "You think I slept with you to stop you from writing the book?"

He glanced back at her but didn't halt. "I couldn't say. I considered the possibility."

"That's low."

"Considering it? Or doing it?"

"I didn't! That's not—" She clamped her mouth shut, her nostrils flaring as she tried to keep up. His legs were longer than hers, dammit. And he wasn't giving an inch.

They reached the bunkhouse. Rio kept going, toward the river. Finally, on the edge of the steep bank, he had to stop.

Meg panted. "It was—it was—only a moment of weakness. I wanted the comfort. That's all. I had no ulterior motive."

But was she being completely honest with herself? A week had passed. She could have brought home a pregnancy test to at least settle that question, however remote the chances were that she'd conceived.

She stared at the churning river. Every morning, there was frost on the banks, icing the crisp rushes into a woven screen. Melted by noon. She felt the same way, her morning's fresh resolve replaced by yearning after a few brief hours with Rio, even when they'd shared no more than a few words or glances.

"A moment of weakness," he repeated. "That's all."

She couldn't respond.

"Huh." He shook his head. "That's not all."

Her gaze slanted toward him. "Are we supposed to pick up where we left off?"

"Of course not."

"And what about your mother? I'm sure she still

disapproves of me. She's going to come here and take one look at us and know…"

"Know what?"

The question was a dare. Meg could see the challenge in his eyes. He wanted her to admit her feelings. But she shook her head, speechless.

"It's obvious that I still care about you," he said, gentler now.

"Caring isn't the issue. You care about the Vaughns."

Rio started to respond, then stopped. With a sigh, he took off his hat and turned it in his hands. Around and around, until Meg felt that her stomach was revolving too, churning endlessly as she waited for him to speak.

His expression was conflicted. "Should I say that I still love you? Is that what you want, Meg? You want me to be the boy who gave you his heart over and over again, even after you'd tuck it away like one of those trinkets in your bedroom, so you could run off with some other guy?"

The hurt she'd caused him was obvious. She recoiled, stung—and guilty. "I'm sorry, Rio. All right? I didn't treat you well. I regret that. But I can't change it, can I? I can't take away the harm I caused."

"I don't care about the fire," he said. "I just want to know if I was ever more to you than the handy guy to keep around. For…" His eyes seemed very black as his lips formed a very cynical smile. "For comfort."

She rubbed her hands, fingers going automatically

to the raised scars on her wrist. "A little comfort isn't such a minor thing."

"It's not enough for me. Not anymore."

There was a quiet desire in his voice that she still couldn't answer, even though her knees almost buckled at the thought of losing him. "Then you probably shouldn't be here."

His face went to stone. "You're asking me to leave?"

"No! Please," she said, humiliatingly imploring.

She wanted him. God, she wanted him. And she probably could have him. But she didn't know how to hold him.

Nor did she deserve him.

"I didn't mean it that way," she said. "Only that you should do what's best for you this time." Her misery was enormous, but she forced the words past it. "And maybe that doesn't include me."

"You've always underestimated yourself."

"Ever wonder if it's you who overestimates me?" She held her head high though her eyes were burning. "What have I ever given you except grief?" She nodded up the slope to the car pulling toward the house. "Your mother knows."

"You gave me friendship. You gave me a home."

"A home?" Meg's laugh was disbelieving. "How can that be when I didn't really have one myself?"

"But you did. Maybe not a perfect one, but you can't deny that Wild River Ranch is your home. You came back here when you needed a sanctuary, didn't you?"

She swallowed. He might be right. She'd always told herself that she had no one but herself to rely on, but hadn't she counted on the ranch, deep in her heart, to be there for her, even though her family no longer was?

Mrs. Carefoot had stepped out of the car. She saw them by the river and lifted a hand, giving a short wave that was neither curt nor enthusiastic. Only cautious.

Rio has a mother and I have a ranch. Meg's hands went to the slight gap in the waistband of her jeans. To create a family, all they needed to find was a father and a child.

Tentatively she touched her flat stomach, wondering if, against all odds, they'd already created both.

"YOU'VE NEVER BEEN to Wild River Ranch before, then?" Meg put the carafe down on a pot holder to protect the cherry-wood dining table.

"Only the times that I drove over to pick up Rio," Virginia Carefoot said. "I never had a tour."

"I guess it's not much compared with the Stones' huge spread."

"It's very—" Virginia glanced around the dining room "—rustic. And this room is nicely set up." Her gaze skimmed along the floorboards.

Meg realized that there were cobwebs clinging to the back edge of the china cabinet. She'd swept now and again—hastily—but the thorough cleaning the place needed was still low on her priority list.

"These were my mother's things," she said of the furnishings and dishes. "Dad left everything exactly as it was. I don't know why. They're just relics."

"Perhaps he valued the memories."

"Or he just didn't want to bother." Meg recognized the gruffness in her tone. "I mean, it's not like he used the stuff. He ate beans cold out of the can."

Not much worse than the way she'd subsisted, before Rio's arrival had domesticated her. Sort of.

Meg lifted her china cup. "He had no use for Royal Doulton." Neither had she, before visitors had started arriving. First the Stones, now Rio's mother. Next it'd be the queen of England. Or perhaps the Vaughns.

She'd have to dust the corners.

"What men would have a use for it?" Rio said with a grin.

"Oh, there's some who do," his mother answered.

He gave a grunt. "No one I know."

Uncomfortably, Meg watched the look they exchanged. Rio had told her they'd never openly discussed his discovery of his parentage, even though he was certain his mother was aware he'd figured it out.

That had been so many years ago. She was amazed they still hadn't talked. If it'd been her, the truth would have come out before long. Probably in an accusation that quickly disintegrated into a raging argument.

Meg picked up the carafe and warmed their coffee before escaping to the kitchen. Mother and son were politely talking about the town's upcoming activities, including the quilt show.

Well, okay. Who was she to say avoidance wasn't the better way to go?

Except that she'd practiced it, too, particularly in recent days. It wasn't working.

RIO WAITED FOR MEG to return from the kitchen, but she didn't come back, even after ten minutes. He wondered if she'd slipped out the front door. The conversation between her and his mother had been polite, but no more. He was disappointed.

After his mother had run through all the local gossip, he ventured a comment. "I was hoping you came here to make peace with Meg."

"My goodness. We've never been at war." Virginia glanced toward the kitchen doorway. "What happened to her?"

"I expect she ducked out to give us some privacy." Rio got up and went to the window in the sitting room. There was Meg, striding up from the barn with her head down and hands thrust into the pockets of her jacket. She got into her car and drove away.

Nice.

THE LATE-AFTERNOON SKY was thick and gray with turbulent clouds. Rio brooded over their argument for a moment before going back to his mother.

"All right," he said. "Let me have it."

Virginia tapped her spoon against the lip of the

coffee cup before carefully setting it on the saucer. She did like to bide her time. Choose her words carefully.

Rio wasn't in the mood. "If it's not Meg, then it must be Stone who sent you here."

"I wasn't sent. But he did mention his visit with you."

"I'm sure he did."

"Naturally, he's concerned about this book of yours."

Rio kept his face from twisting into a sneer. "And since he got nowhere with me, he goes ahead and enlists my mother?"

"I realize how prestigious it would be to be published. We just wish you'd consider the aftermath."

"We?"

Virginia's frown deepened. "The Stones are as concerned as I am."

"I didn't realize the senator's wife was in Treetop." Of course she wasn't. Mrs. Stone was a rare visitor, preferring D.C. and other points east of Wyoming.

Virginia's chin firmed. "I meant Lissy and Billy. They're concerned for their father. His health hasn't been good."

"Anything serious?"

"A bout with colitis. It's under control. Billy's been taking over the reins at the ranch."

"Good old Billy. I suppose he's also been putting in his two cents' on my book." Sticking his nose in was more like it.

"Don't be snide. Billy's really made something of

himself. He has his own real estate investment company."

A rigid contrariness crept into Rio's neck and shoulders. "Making the old man proud, huh? And not by writing a tell-all book."

"Rio," his mother admonished. "Never think that I'm not proud of you."

"Yeah." He sighed. "You are."

An uncomfortable silence grew between them, one that was as old as he was. For an amorphous thing it was heavy and solid and real. A boulder on his shoulders that he wanted to heave far away.

"You're my son," his mother said softly. "I'll always be proud of you."

"If I publish the book?"

She took a breath. "Even then."

"I doubt that's what Stone wanted you to say."

A wry smile tipped up the corners of his mother's mouth. "You're mistaken if you believe I don't have a mind of my own."

"Oh, I'm sure you do. It just seems to me he has more influence than he should."

Virginia shook her head. When she spoke, it was clear that the slight opening he'd sensed in her defenses was closed. "I could say the same about you—with Meg. She's back in your life and already you two are in trouble."

Rio hesitated. His mother had never understood that Meg had been his release from the unspoken tensions at the Stone ranch, tensions he'd barely understood but felt all the same. With Meg, he was free. For a number of years, that freedom had been a sweet, innocent, joyful thing. Only when they'd grown older, seventeen, eighteen, had her wild streak taken a turn into the realm of the dangerous and the criminal, of the misdemeanor sort.

Any trouble she'd caused had been worth the price.

But was he willing to keep paying?

"You mean the vandalism?" he asked his mother. "Are you blaming Meg or me for that?"

"Of course I'm not blaming you." She appeared unusually uncomfortable, fidgeting with her hands and twisting her ring. "I'm just saying that maybe this is a sign that things are not right."

"According to whom?" he asked. "Not me."

Virginia put her hands in her lap. "I shouldn't have said anything."

Rio got a strange feeling. "Do you know something? Is that why you're here?"

"It's just a visit. A nice visit."

Not so nice as that.

"But maybe you ought to be careful," she added with a frown.

"You do know something." Lissy or Billy? Rio wondered. Stone? All seemed highly unlikely when he'd been so certain that the vandal was the mean-spirited Vaughn. Perhaps it was time to call in the police.

Virginia left soon after, unwilling to say more even when he pressed her. Her loyalty to the Stones might have been admirable under other circumstances. In this case, it left Rio feeling that he had no one in his corner. He couldn't even be sure of Meg.

Ten minutes later, she drove up, her car sounding like a rattletrap on the rough driveway. He'd been waiting for her on the front porch, sitting on the low fieldstone wall, but he stood to greet her.

"Thanks for disappearing," he said as she got out of the car.

"Sarcasm? From you? I must have really ticked you off."

"At least you could have said you were leaving."

"Sorry. I thought you two would like some time alone." Meg had gotten out of the car and opened the back door. She reached in and fiddled with a bulky item in the backseat.

"Maybe this will make up for it," she said with a tentative smile. "I brought you a present."

She walked toward him, cradling a sleeping puppy to her chest. "I hope it's okay that I picked the female. Her name's Gabby. She was talking to me nonstop on the way home, but apparently all that whimpering and whining tuckered the poor girl out. She's zonked."

Meg put the puppy in his hands. "The Vaughns said hello."

He stroked the puppy's head. "Thanks. But are you sure she belongs to me?"

Meg threw up her hands. "What would I do with a puppy?"

Love it, he thought. *Since you can't love me.*

CHAPTER TWELVE

FOUR DAYS LATER, Meg could no longer deny that Gabby was her dog. While Rio made a token effort to keep the puppy occupied, whenever he was working elsewhere Gabby followed Meg around the barn and the house, constantly underfoot. Eventually she gave up shooing the puppy away because if Gabby wasn't with her, that likely meant the little terrier was off making mischief. Overturning buckets. Shredding a corner of the feed sack, spilling oats across the floor. Finding and hiding every sock, glove and piece of underwear in the house. At one point Meg had convinced Rio to shut Gabby into his cabin for the afternoon, but one hour of yips so piercing they could be heard all over the ranch had put a fast end to that experiment.

After a full week of togetherness, Meg had to admit she enjoyed the puppy's company. They conversed, once she'd learned how to interpret the various whimpers and barks. The puppy learned that "Gabby, no!" was far more serious than a "G-a-abby, no-o-o!"

Even Axxaashe and the other horses had grown accustomed to the puppy, whether Gabby was shooting out at them across the corral or curled up sleeping in the stall, burrowed into the bedding so deeply the pup was invisible to Meg, but never her stablemates. As the mustang's groundwork progressed into longer mounted rides around the corral, Gabby became a stowaway, deposited safely out of hoof reach in a pair of saddlebags strapped across the mare's back.

"C'mere, tiny terror. We're going for a ride." Meg scooped up the puppy and tucked her beneath the bag's leather flap before mounting. Gabby whimpered and squirmed, finally thrusting her nose out of the bag, blinking at Meg from beneath her fringed brow. Axxaashe gave only an impatient snort.

"You can open it," Meg called to Rio. He was watching from the gate, ready at hand in case the mare's first foray out of the round pen turned hairy.

"Shouldn't I take the puppy?"

"She's less bother staying put where I can keep an eye on her."

"But if Axx decides to act badly…"

"She won't." Meg reached to stroke the mare's strawberry-speckled neck, grown sleek from a healthy diet and rigorous grooming. "Axx is a real sweetheart."

Not exactly. But the mustang had progressed so rapidly from the bolting auction reject to a reasonably well-behaved mount that Rio had suggested they call the BLM to track down her history through the freeze mark. So far, Meg had resisted. Some histories shouldn't be dug up.

Rio swung open the gate.

"We're not going far," Meg promised as the mare stepped warily through the opening. Axxaashe's head was high, her ears alert and flickering as she minced along the frozen ground. Taking a spill on the hard surface would hurt, but then Meg had no intention of doing something so ignominious.

And, potentially, disastrous.

She clenched the braided rope reins. *No fear. I'm not knocked up.*

She could tell herself that all she wanted, but there was still a chance, even if it was only the extreme unlikelihood of a million-to-one shot. She hadn't yet had the opportunity to use the pregnancy test she'd just that morning brought home from a drugstore in Rawlins, which was a thirty-five-minute drive from home and therefore far enough away for people to mind their own business. She'd had to wait a week before finding a reasonable excuse—an end-of-the-season sale at the saddlery store—for getting out of town.

Attuned to her rider's distress, the mustang capered sideways, her head yawing as she tried to take in all her surroundings at once.

Meg soothed the mare with a few low-spoken words before straightening her out and propelling her forward with a light leg squeeze. "Come on, girl. Let's show him what we've got."

"The Wild River Angels," Rio said with a smile as the trio of females headed toward the open field, an easy stretch of ochre stubble.

Meg cocked a brow. "Devils, more like."

"Reformed," he replied, adding under his breath, "I hope."

He could have been referring to any of them. "Me or the horse?" Meg asked over her shoulder.

"Both of you." He tsked. "Keep your attention where it belongs."

She snapped her gaze back to the mare's ears, pricked in the direction of the open range. "We're doing fine."

She nudged Axxaashe into a slow trot. They'd take a couple of turns around the pasture, following the new board fence Rio had been putting up. Nothing bad would happen, even with him practically scowling at them the entire time.

The ride went well. Gabby stayed put and so did Meg, making herself a steadying presence for the skittery mare. She kept Rio out of her mind as much as possible and concentrated on the horse, executing several stops and starts, easy circles and gait changes.

They did so well, and ignored Rio so completely, that Meg was surprised to find him gone when she rode back toward the barn. A familiar car was parked nearby.

Meg's heart sank. "Super," she said, even before hearing the also-familiar laughter coming from inside the barn. The frequency of female visitors to the ranch had tripled in the past week, if you could triple zero.

Meg dismounted, then liberated Gabby from the saddlebag. The puppy scurried into the barn and was greeted by a squeal of delight. Today it was Lissy Stone. Yesterday had been Julie Engstrom, ostensibly checking up on the progress of her Arab, which had only been in residence for two days and therefore had made no measurable progress, as Meg had pointed out through gritted teeth. It didn't take a genius to recognize the ranch's real appeal.

Meg grumbled, "Just super." Axxaashe was still not comfortable as a stable horse, so she unsaddled and groomed the mare at an outside hitching post.

Not that I begrudge Rio a half sister, she told herself as she applied the curry comb to the strawberry roan.

Lissy had seemed nice enough on her first visit. Still had the air of entitlement that both Rio and Meg used to find disgusting, but she didn't appear spiteful. Rio treated her with a cautious welcome.

Meg worried, all the same. She knew better than anyone what it was to lack a family. How big that hole could feel. How unfillable.

At least Rio's mother had been there for him, even if Virginia's choices had limited her son's. For Meg, there'd only been her dad, who hadn't shown any affection at all.

A sense of guilt niggled at her. Was she being less than generous? Her dad hadn't been an ideal father, neither supportive nor demonstrative, but he'd given her a home. He'd cared…some. Or he had, until she'd rejected both him and the ranch by running away. And staying away. Without a word, except for one measly ninety-nine-cent Christmas card when she was at a low point.

A card he'd saved.

It was likely that she'd hurt him as much as he'd hurt her. No wonder, she reluctantly admitted, his stubborn pride wouldn't let him welcome her home, even from his deathbed.

Meg scoffed. "What a messed-up couple of jackasses."

Lissy's laugh made Meg jump. "Really, Meg! She might not be a thoroughbred, but she's looking a lot better than the scruffy old nag I saw on my last visit."

Meg gave the mare a reassuring stroke. "Axxaashe's no nag. All she needed was TLC."

Lissy dropped her voice. "Rio, too. Am I right?"

"I wouldn't know."

"Sure you would."

Meg glanced sidelong at the woman, dressed as impractically as ever in a belted white leather coat and designer boots with stiletto heels. Lissy's smugness was irritating. But it was her sleek style and utter confidence that got under Meg's skin and made her feel inadequate.

She tugged at the frayed sleeves of her denim jacket. Old wounds.

"No, I don't," Meg said. "Why does everyone assume that Rio and I are taking up where we left off? It's been a decade. Maybe our past is as cold as the grave."

An overly vehement but not-bad spiel. Except for the maybe.

Lissy arched a brow. "I see you still haven't mellowed out."

"Sorry." Meg looked toward the barn for Rio, but he was nowhere to be seen. "It's just that there have been a few too many insinuating grins aimed our way. And then his mother visits…"

"She did?"

"You didn't know? I thought your father sent her."

"That could be. I'm not in the loop these days."

"What loop?"

"Oh, you know how it is with men." Lissy waved a hand. "My father and Billy always have their little plans."

Meg didn't care for the sound of that. "So. When do we have the pleasure of a visit from Billy? I assume he's next."

Lissy shrugged. "He's a busy boy these days."

Quickly Meg ran a cloth over her horse, then led the mare around to the corral and set her loose. The Dutch door remained open, but Axxaashe still hadn't come inside even though she'd grown curious enough to poke her nose in now and then, especially at feeding time.

Meg walked back to Lissy, bare hands plunged into her jacket pockets. They were clenched so hard she could feel her pulse.

She stared. Lissy was shivering inside her quilted coat.

"Are you really here to make up to Rio?" Meg demanded. "Do you actually want him as a brother?" She inhaled sharply. "Because if you're not, if you have other motives and are taking advantage of him, that's just plain cruel."

Lissy blinked. "I am not cruel."

"What about your father? I bet you'd do anything he asked."

"I would not."

"You ignored Rio all these years. You and Billy both."

"I wasn't there! And then he was gone, in the army. What was I supposed to do?"

"You could have contacted him. He might have liked to know that you cared, even a little."

Meg almost flinched, hearing her own words. Was she mad at Lissy, or herself?

"I didn't think he wanted that. His mother didn't." Lissy's face had crumpled. "I approached her, years ago. I—I tried to bring up the subject. She just turned her back and wouldn't respond. She shut me down."

Meg could imagine that happening, easily. Rio's mother was the center spoke of the entire cover-up, even more than William Walker Stone. She'd allowed her son to be shunted aside.

"Then I tried with my father," Lissy continued. "He's heavily into denial." She took on a mocking tone. "'I did not have sex with that woman.'"

Meg could only shake her head.

Lissy appealed to her, clutching at her arm with gloved hands. "What else was I supposed to do? Tell me and I'll try it."

"I don't know." Meg heard Rio talking to the puppy inside the barn. "But there must be something."

Something to heal all of us, she thought hopelessly. There were no easy solutions.

Inviting Lissy and Rio up to the house to get warm seemed like a tiny first step.

THAT EVENING, the phone in the hallway rang while Meg and Rio were just sitting down to dinner. She got up to answer it and he listened blatantly, especially after her voice took on the reserved tone she used with strangers.

"Yes, he's here. I'll get—"

The caller interrupted.

"I suppose I used to be," Meg responded pricklishly. "If that's how you want to label me."

Rio smiled to himself. What would Meg be without her quills?

The answer tugged at his gut. She'd be the kind of woman he'd had in bed, that one night when she'd let down her guard long enough to make love. A woman capable of real warmth and caring. A woman he could love. Not in the way he'd loved her as a girl, when their relationship had been so new and tentative.

A deeper, more meaningful love.

"It's for you." Meg stood in the doorway, holding out the phone. "A woman named Higgins."

He took the phone, an old model with a heavy hand-set and a coiled, knotted cord. "My agent."

Meg slipped past him, avoiding his glance. "I'll give you privacy."

He walked into the hall. "Hi, Jane."

"Loved the proposal," the literary agent said without preamble. "I'm sending it out at once. We'll start with three of the top publishers. I've already had a nibble from Norseman. Then the others will be dying for a look and before you know it, we'll have a feeding frenzy. One can hope."

"What?"

"With any luck, we'll have a bidding war. The only problem I see is that Afghanistan isn't the hot topic these days. That's why I'm thrilled with the pages from your early years. All that turmoil and angst! Young lovers torn apart by cruel fate—and fathers. That'll always sell."

"Hold on, now. Let me catch my breath."

"That was her? Meg? Is she pretty?"

"She's—um. What did you call her when she was on the phone?"

"Before? I don't remember. Never mind, we'll use a full back-cover photo of you looking especially rugged and that'll draw in the readers like nobody's biz. It works for Sebastian Junger."

"I'm not—"

"I spoke too soon. There is another problem, poten-tially. Some big-shot lawyer has been contacting ed-itors, warning them away from the memoir with threats of lawsuits." Jane laughed. "Which could spell trouble in the future, but for now the ploy has only served to whet their appetites."

"Who…?"

"The scandal will be delish, if we can find a sexy angle. A shame that Stone's so old and not that well known anymore. Wyoming's not a hotbed of sex appeal either, but we'll work with what we have. We can run with the ride-a-cowboy thing."

"Sexy angle," Rio echoed in disbelief.

"Now, if you and Meg hooked up again—that'd be ideal. Pure schmaltz, of course, but it'd sell to the housewives in Boise. You didn't say, is she pretty?"

Rio walked the length of the cord. Meg wasn't in the kitchen.

"Your silence does not bode well," Jane said.

"Don't worry. Meg's striking." Yep. She'd strike damn fast if she were privy to the agent's viewpoint. "She's definitely not the type to participate in any publicity, if that's what you're thinking."

"Let's not jump the gun. Still, it doesn't hurt to have a few options lined up."

"Not Meg."

"We'll see."

"Meg's not negotiable."

Jane laughed. "I can believe that. She didn't sound cooperative."

"I'm not sure if I am, either. What's this about sexy angles?"

"That's for me to figure. You just sit tight, cowboy. Carry your cell while you're out riding fence or busting broncs. I'll call back as soon as I've gotten the first response."

The agent hung up. Rio stood in the dim hallway, looking at the phone, trying to process the conversation. He'd met Jane Higgins once, in New York City, a side trip worked in between his official discharge and his trip west to Treetop. With Jane having already read selections from his blog, their meeting had gone much faster than he'd anticipated. She'd scrutinized him in a matter of seconds, pronounced him her client and sent him on his way with instructions to churn out some pages for her ASAP.

He'd e-mailed an outline and sample pages two days ago. There'd be time, he'd assumed, to work up to telling Meg that the deal was in the works. The worry over Stone and his lawyer weaseling their way into the publishing houses was another problem he'd deal with later.

For now, he only wanted to absorb the astonishing news that the process was moving much faster than he'd expected.

He stood with his hands clasped at the back of his head. Nope. Even that was too much to wrap his mind around.

He heard Meg coming in the back door with Gabby and went to greet them. She was scolding the dog for peeing on the linoleum.

Meg peeled off her jacket and hung it on the back of a chair. "Your agent?" she asked, coolly surveying the table. "That sounds so Hollywood."

"I know. I'm not used to saying it."

"She called me your love interest. Your Juliet." Meg snorted. "I hope that doesn't mean I have to drink poison. Or was it Juliet who used the dagger?"

"Jane's a saleswoman." The puppy came over and plopped herself onto the toe of Rio's boot. He picked her up and held her against his chest, her back legs peddling until he gathered them up.

"She's not selling me," Meg said with vehemence.

There were two ways to take that. He decided that either way was the wrong one, at least for now. Especially when he wasn't even ready to believe that a book deal was actually pending, Jane Higgins's total confidence notwithstanding.

"Not selling me out," Meg muttered as she picked up their plates and stuck them in the microwave one at a time.

"I wouldn't—" He stopped midsentence. He wouldn't do that? Ha. He was doing exactly that.

Meg looked at him, her forehead crinkled. "What's the deal?"

He was startled. Perhaps guilty. "There's no deal."

"I meant—what's up? It's past nine o'clock in New York. Not the usual business hours."

"I think Jane works all hours."

The microwave beeped on the second plate. Meg set

it on the table, using the edge of her sleeve as a pot holder. "So she wasn't calling about anything special."

"I e-mailed her the proposal for the memoir. She liked it."

"Oh, wow. That's…" Meg sat abruptly. "Congratulations. I guess."

He put the puppy down and went to wash his hands at the kitchen sink. The cover of running water made it easier to add, "She's already working on a book deal."

"That's fast. I thought you had to write the entire book first."

"Not always." He dried his hands, being deliberate about it. He didn't want to turn around and face Meg with the truth—that he was, basically, selling out both her and his mother. Of all the people in his life, they were the only ones he cared about, even though the thought of exposing the Stones also gave him some remorse. Lissy had become something of a friend, if not actually a sister. He even had some sympathy for the old man and his vaunted legacy.

But not enough to give up a book deal. He'd already paid his share of the blame by allowing himself to be railroaded into the army. Now it was their turn.

Meg was sitting with her chin propped on one hand. Her dinner remained untouched. "This is really happening."

Rio rejoined her. "I don't believe it. Not yet."

Gabby whimpered, tired of waiting for a tidbit to fall. Meg sliced off a minuscule shred of ham and fed it to the puppy off her fingertips. Rio shook his head, but she shrugged. "It's a celebration, right? You're about to become an author. Too bad there's no wine. We should have a toast."

"It's too early for that." He doubted he'd be celebrating anyway, which was suddenly a telling point. If he couldn't celebrate even if a deal went down, there was obviously something rotten at the heart of it.

"You should be proud, anyway," Meg said. The wariness in her eyes gave her away. She looked down. "I didn't really doubt that this would happen, especially after I read some of what you'd written. I'm just not sure I wanted it to happen."

She drew in a breath. "But I should have. You deserve success and I ought to feel happy for you."

"I understand—"

"No. It's time for me to be the understanding one." Meg stood and gave him a brief hug. Her lips touched his forehead. "I wish you the best, Rio. Honestly."

She would have retreated, but he wouldn't let her go. He wound his arms around her waist and pressed his face to her abdomen, inhaling raggedly as the same old desire hit him hard. He'd kept his distance to let Meg adjust to the idea of them being together again. But she'd gone on as if nothing had happened between them. Knowing her, she could continue that way forever, giving in to brief encounters she'd pretend were aberrations.

And that wasn't going to cut it for him. Not anymore.

"I don't know what to do," he said huskily. This was about more than the book.

After a moment's hesitation, she smoothed down his hair with her hands. She sighed. "Just tell the truth."

He looked up at her. "And let the chips fall where they may?"

She lowered her face to his. Their foreheads touched. "You're not responsible for the consequences."

"Even yours?"

"I'm tough. I can deal with it."

His fingers circled one of her wrists, finding the narrow line of scar tissue. "I'm not so sure about that."

She stiffened against him. "That was a long time ago. I'm a lot stronger now." Her face knotted as if pulled taut by a rope. "A lot stronger. Believe me, I've survived worse than a moment of drunken self-pity."

Rio stood, catching her hands as she dropped them. "But are you ready to face all of our past?" And could she forgive him for exposing her?

Her eyes were slightly red, but he saw conviction in them. She gripped him, squeezed his hands together as if she could make him hold strong through force of will. "This is your chance, Rio. You have to take it. I won't ever forgive you if you don't."

He shook his head. "Now I'm the one who needs redemption?"

A small smile tugged at the corners of her lips. "All right then. I'll think that you haven't forgiven me."

He gave her a quick, soft kiss, his mouth hovering

against her trembling lower lip. She caught her breath, then released it with a shaky sigh. "I told you," he said. "There's nothing to forgive."

She shut her eyes. "Of course there is."

"That's over. It was over, like you said, a long time ago."

"That doesn't mean all is forgiven. Or forgotten."

"It can be. We just have to let it go."

"After you write it," she said.

He relented, saying, "Yes," before kissing her. "I want to make love to you."

She pulled back. "Oh, Rio. That's a complication we don't need."

He moved closer. "Celebrate with me."

"It's not enough that I'm pleading with you to write the damn book? Now I have to celebrate, too?" She pushed against his chest as he pressed her into the cabinets.

He lifted her onto the countertop and moved into position between her legs. Kissing her with unmistakable intent, he wedged one hand at the back of her thigh. "Sweet girl, I've run out of patience."

Her moan was half protest, half pleasure. "Sweet?"

He strung kisses along her neck.

"I'm not sweet," she protested, arching her throat against his lips.

"Oh, yes, you are, Meggie Jo. You've always been sweet and sour. Like cherries." She wrapped her legs around his waist as he lifted her and headed for the bedroom. "It's just that I'm the only one who sees it."

CHAPTER THIRTEEN

A RAINBOW OF TUMBLING blocks spilled from one corner of the suspended quilt to the other. Meg stood in the small crowd attending the quilt show and stared until the colors blurred.

She blinked. Her vision didn't clear until she dashed at her eyes with the edge of the long scarf knotted around her neck. Only then did she realize that she'd been crying.

Again.

She wanted to be disgusted with herself. The Vegas Meg would have been. Same with the teenage Meg. But this new Meg was, amazingly, cutting herself some slack.

Returning to Wild River Ranch had proven to be even more emotional than she'd feared. She hadn't cried this much in the hospital after her last miscarriage, having lost first her relationship with Jase and then her months-old fetus. After the initial examination and tests, her doctor had said that while conceiving was unlikely, carrying a baby to term would be virtually impossible. He'd wanted Meg to book an appointment for further diagnosis, but she'd heard enough.

And taken enough punishment.

One week, two weeks. She counted on her fingers. Exactly fifteen days since she'd initially slept with Rio. She'd managed to avoid explaining that she didn't have to use birth control because she probably couldn't conceive anyway. The pregnancy-test kit still waited in a plastic bag tucked under a stack of towels in the linen closet. She hadn't dared use it.

Hoping was better when the knowledge wasn't what you wanted to hear. She felt pitiful admitting it, but wishing was all she had left.

She hadn't clung to such foolish dreams since she'd left home thinking that a rich new world was hers for the asking. Then, she'd had an excuse. Most eighteen-year-olds had outsize expectations.

Now, it was time to accept reality.

Yes. Absolutely. She'd take the test today, right after she got home.

The stitching on the quilt was meticulous. The colors were lovely. But she knew she could never quilt the way her mother had. Merely thinking of the hours of monotonous work made her feel claustrophobic. She couldn't imagine the tedium of being stuck in the gloomy ranch house through an endless winter, marking every minute of every day, stitch by painstaking stitch. No wonder her mother had gone a little nuts.

"It's a beautiful quilt."

The appearance of Virginia Carefoot, in a woolen

kerchief and unzipped red parka, gave Meg's stomach
a turn. Especially since she'd skipped out on the woman's recent visit to the ranch. Bringing home a puppy
hadn't been quite excuse enough.

"My mother's," Meg said with tentative pride.

"I didn't know she was a quilter."

"I'd forgotten, too, but Mrs. Briggs—" Queenie's
mother, who'd organized the show "—called to ask if
I'd loan her a quilt. She remembered that my mother
had joined a group of local seamstresses to learn how
her second year on the ranch. She made several quilts,
maybe the first projects she actually completed from
start to finish. I found them packed away in an old
cedar chest in the attic." Her father hadn't touched the
quilts. Sad...but predictable.

Meg cleared her throat. "I've been remembering
how she used to work on them all winter, stitching dili-
gently every night after dinner."

Virginia looked closely. "Completely hand-sewn.
That's amazing."

Meg studied the geometric blocks, noticing how
carefully the colors had been chosen, the precise stitching around every edge. "I wouldn't have the patience."

You'd have to be obsessed, she thought.

"Quilting requires quite an investment of time and
dedication." Virginia nodded. "There's no instant grat-
ification to it."

"Must be a dying art then." Meg tried to speak as if
she didn't care. She wouldn't have, even a few years

ago. Now, she saw some value in longevity. In going the distance.

She'd never gone any distance except when she was running away.

"I could never, never do it," she said.

Virginia smiled. "There'll come a time when you learn to appreciate a slower pace of life."

Meg's initial reaction was to deny that, which was just plain mulishness. She wasn't the wild young kid she'd been, after all. She was nearly thirty.

"Rio's not with you?"

"No. There was work to do around the barn and then he was going to see to Gig, over at the Vaughns'." Something as simple as using the name of her elderly neighbors out loud had once been an embarrassment to her, but she'd grown used to that, had acknowledged her guilt and the gossip she'd caused. She'd even learned to accept the Vaughns' forgiveness, and with a small amount of grace, too.

"How much longer do you expect you'll need him?" Virginia asked carefully. Clearly still hoping that Meg would loosen her hold.

How long will I need Rio? she asked herself. Easy answer.

Forever.

But his mother had other ideas. Meg pressed her lips together. "He can work for me as long as he cares to. He's free to go anytime."

"It's a stopgap then."

"For him or for me?" *Or both of us,* she silently added with a sense of roiling dread.

Last night, Rio had touched her with real tenderness. But she wasn't counting on it being love.

Virginia was looking across the room at a man who seemed naggingly familiar to Meg. Tall, stockily muscular, dark blond hair wet-combed back from a face that was handsome, if a bit florid around the bulging jaw. He was sharply dressed in a three-piece suit that seemed out of place among the other guys' Wranglers overalls.

She couldn't place the man until he laughed—a high-pitched titter that she felt in her vertebrae, like the call of a coyote.

"What's Billy Stone doing here?" she asked Virginia.

Maybe he's different, she told herself. Improved. Like Lissy. But just looking at him, glad-handing a rancher as if they were old friends, told her otherwise. "Is he running for office?"

"Looks like it, doesn't it?" Virginia seemed to have no more use for Billy than Meg. "I suppose he's trolling for opportunities."

Meg watched him hand out a couple of flyers from a stack on the booth beside him. Several vendors had set up to take advantage of the quilt-show traffic—an insurance company, a few arts and crafters, the local VFW selling candy bars. Billy's booth featured a toothy redhead and a bright green banner with a triangular logo. Peak Properties.

Meg felt uneasy. "That's right. His sister mentioned he's gone into business."

"He claims to already own half of Treetop," Virginia said. "Including mineral rights. I hope that's not true."

"Even if he does, what's he going to do with it?"

"Sulfide mining is the rumor. Geologists, surveyors and other experts have been checking in and out of the Stone ranch like it's a motel."

"That sounds ominous."

"A big mining operation would create many jobs for the town," Virginia pointed out.

"I guess."

Billy had spotted them. He waved, gesturing that they should come over to join him.

Virginia crossed her arms. "He wants you."

"Me?" Meg didn't enjoy being summoned by the likes of Billy Jr., but she was curious enough to saunter across the room, an auditorium in the Treetop Town Hall. The colorful quilts hung from racks that effectively divided the space into several long aisles. The Peak Properties booth was against the far wall, flanked by the American and Wyoming State flags.

Meg held out her hand to Billy. All hail the chief.

"Meg Lennox, I thought that was you." Billy pumped her hand vigorously. "You look just the same."

"I can't say you do."

"Luckily." He tugged at his collar, knotted a bit too high and tight by an expensive silk tie. "I was a tub as a kid." He took in her boots and jeans, the jacket that smelled like the barn. "What's it been? Nine, ten years?"

"A long time."

"You're still stunning."

Billy's blue eyes were appreciative, though she'd never got the feeling that she was his type. She'd only met him a few times after they were older. He'd been a preppie by then, less chubby and grasping but with an even greater sense of entitlement, the type of guy who thought that hometown girls who'd stayed at home were really kind of dull.

"You inherited the ranch?"

He'd made that a question, but she suspected he knew very well she had. Wouldn't have surprised her if he'd even looked up the legal documents of transfer.

She shrugged. "There was no one else."

"Got any plans for the place?"

Again, she guessed he already knew what she was doing. "I'm running a horse-training and boarding business."

Billy gave her a broad smile. "How's that going for you?"

"Slowly," she admitted.

"Well, I wish you the best. But if you're ever interested in selling, I'm buying." Billy gave her one of the brochures. "Peak Properties. You can find all my contact information in there. Give us a call anytime."

He turned away. Meg retreated, feeling summarily dismissed when she'd been expecting the hard sell. She walked straight to the exit, not stopping, exchanging only brief nods with the few people who recognized her.

I should be glad. I don't want to sell anyway.

But she had to wonder. How had Billy managed to miss the golden opportunity to snatch the ranch when her father's health had been failing?

"MEG?" RIO CALLED even though he sensed the house was empty. Her car was outside, but she wasn't in the barn either. He put Gabby down. The puppy let out one sharp bark and scurried down the hall.

"Gabby, c'mere." Rio followed the dog, intending to take her with him to the cabin. Meg couldn't have gone far.

The little terrier had jumped onto Meg's unmade bed. He booted her off. She nosed under the dust ruffle, coming out with a leather glove that already bore teeth marks. She flipped it up into the air, then pounced on it with a growl.

Rio rescued the glove then picked up the red scarf that Meg had worn that morning on her way into town.

Gabby snapped at the knotted fringe. Rio gathered it up and tossed it on the bed. Meg wasn't the most vigilant housekeeper at any time, but she must have been in a rush when she'd returned from the quilt show. He'd been slightly surprised that she'd wanted to go in the first place. Maybe she was finally feeling more at home in Treetop.

Gabby caught the end of the scarf and dragged it off

the bed. Rio grabbed the other end and tugged lightly. "Gabby, no."

During their tussle, the glove fell off the bed. Gabby abandoned the scarf to pounce on it again. She snatched it up and trotted out of the room, tail wriggling, holding the glove high.

Rio gave chase. "Gabby. come here." He tried to catch her, but she darted into the bathroom across the hall.

Lightning quick, Gabby dropped the glove to upset the trash can instead. She tossed a tissue into the air.

"Rascal." Rio was about to clean up the mess when the sight of an emptied pink and white box stopped him. Bold letters spelled out Expectations across the front of it. Some brand name. Sounded like…

He examined the box. *When you're expecting the unexpected. Know for certain within minutes!*

Rio groaned out loud. Meg was pregnant.

Was Meg pregnant?

He felt as if he'd taken a punch. All the air had left his lungs. He looked for the test stick in the trash, around the sink, in Meg's bedroom. Nothing.

Back in the bathroom, Gabby was shredding tissues with abandon. He picked her up. Her tiny nose twitched. "Where's Meg?" he asked. *What's she done?*

The questions were pounding at his brain. She'd said there was nothing to worry about. He'd believed her.

Had she lied?

Suddenly, the silence in the house seemed ominous.

He tossed the box into the trash can and jogged outside with Gabby tucked under his arm. A second tour of the barn proved that all horses were accounted for except the mustang. He checked outside. The gate to the round pen was open. Okay, so she'd gone for a ride. No need to worry.

Several anxious minutes later, he heard hoof beats. Relief washed through him, only to be replaced by the shock of finding the pregnancy test. Meg wouldn't like being questioned, but this time he was going to get an answer.

Except something was wrong. Meg didn't appear. He went outside and discovered Axxaashe, wandering loose with an empty saddle and trailing reins. The horse shied away from him and went totting along the corral fence.

Meg had been unseated. Adrenaline pumped into Rio's veins at the possibility of her being injured. Without conscious decision, he reacted with swift efficiency, herding the mustang into the corral, shutting Gabby into a box stall, saddling Renny and galloping away from the barn. Meg wouldn't have gone far on the mustang, but there was no way of knowing— if she'd been tossed—how serious her injuries might be.

The frozen ground thudded beneath his mount's pounding hooves. Rio scanned the fields, hoping to see a ticked-off Meg striding toward him. She was no stranger to taking falls. Hell, as a kid, she'd even courted the spills, riding bareback like a banshee with her hair whipping in the wind.

The home pasture was empty. He pointed Renny toward the foothills. The ranch land was stark in the cold, bright sunshine. He pulled up his mount, the stillness broken only by his own heavy breathing and a snort from the horse.

"Meg?" he called. No answer.

He urged Renny on. "Meg?"

The land rose past a line of craggy rock. A movement there caught his eye and with a kick he put his horse into a lope. He swung off before they'd stopped.

Meg's white face appeared from the other side of the rocks. She braced an arm against one of the stones and pushed herself up to a sitting position.

He was at her side in seconds. "Are you all right?"

"Sure." She groaned. "I'm just an idiot."

She tried to rise, but quickly sat back down. He knelt, easing her into his arms. "Don't move yet. Are you hurt?"

"Only my pride, as they say." She laughed shakily. "Really, I'm okay. But I do have a wicked headache. My head bounced off the ground."

"Maybe you need an ambulance."

"For what?" She looked up from picking dirt out of her palms. "I'm fine. It was just a fall."

"Were you knocked out?"

"Nope. Momentarily stunned. And royally peeved that Axx took off on me. Did she go back to the barn?"

"She's there. I put her in the corral. Don't move," he barked when Meg again tried to get up. Her pale face was scaring him. He'd never known her not to bounce up immediately after a tumble. She had to be hurting more than she'd admit.

"I can't just sit here." She sounded agitated. "The ground is cold."

He ripped off his jacket and slid it beneath her. "What happened?"

She grunted. "I was going too fast. Something made Axx shy and I kind of slid off."

"You didn't just slide off."

"More or less." Meg touched the back of her skull and winced. "But the ground was uneven and I lost my balance."

He pushed her hair back from the spot she'd been probing. "There's no blood. But you've got a helluva bump. Let me see your eyes."

She widened them. "Are you a doctor now?"

"I know some first aid." Seeing the direct steadiness of her gaze, he said a quick, silent prayer. She was typically defiant, maybe more so whenever she felt vulnerable. "Your pupils are even. That's good."

"I have a hard head."

He checked over her legs as best he could through her jeans and boots. "What about the rest of you?"

"Hard as nails." She raked a hand through her hair, wincing again.

His sympathy was gradually losing ground to the

questions he had for her. But he couldn't interrogate her right now. Even so, he had to ask, "You sure about that?"

She narrowed her eyes. "What do you mean?"

"Just checking. You're absolutely sure you're not—"

"I said I'm fine." She extended a hand. "But you can help me up."

He put his hands around her waist and eased her onto her feet. "Maybe there are, um, internal injuries."

With an impatient yank, she adjusted her jacket. "From one small fall? I doubt it."

"A hard fall."

"What's with you, Rio? You're fussing like a grandma."

"Well, you're not a teenager anymore."

She brushed off the seat of her pants. "Just get my old bones back to the house."

"You're sure you're okay?" he asked again as he prepared to help her aboard Renny. "Maybe you shouldn't be riding."

She pulled back her head, giving him a sharp look. "Why not?"

"Same reason you were riding recklessly in the first place."

She wore an expression of disbelief, as if he were acting crazy. Perhaps he was. He didn't know how to negotiate these particular turbulent waters.

"What's that supposed to mean?" she asked slowly.

He gave up hoping that she'd be straightforward with him. "Enough, Meg. Just tell me. Are you pregnant?"

CHAPTER FOURTEEN

"I'M NOT PREGNANT. I'll never be pregnant again," she'd snapped bitterly.

Rio didn't deserve to bear the brunt of her pain over discovering that she was not expecting. But she hadn't been able to stop herself.

He'd been stunned, of course. Confused. He'd asked her why she'd been using a test kit in the first place. The explanation was too much for her. She'd taken off on foot and had refused to talk to Rio all the way back to the ranch. After several attempts to get her to open up, he'd grown exasperated and had given in to his own aggrieved feelings about being kept in the dark.

In stony silence they'd put the horses away, watered and fed them. Meg had walked out before the work was done, then returned and rescued Gabby.

She needed every bit of comfort available.

She didn't make dinner. And Rio didn't come looking for it.

But he was in the cabin—the light was on. Meg took a couple of ibuprofen and stood at the window, drinking a glass of water. She was sorry for giving him the cold shoulder. Her disappointment wasn't his fault. Not even the memory of that time long ago. He'd been shut out then, too.

It hurt to face the truth: that she'd never allowed him in. Not really.

Had he always recognized that?

I'm not pregnant. I'll never be pregnant again.

She hadn't wanted to face it until now. And naturally Rio had the right to question her since she'd misled him about the need to use birth control, even though he'd had no business picking through her garbage.

Like she'd gone through his manuscript.

The sun had dipped below the mountains. Slowly, the violets, pinks and grays of the western sky deepened to purple.

Last light.

She watched the cabin until Rio's light went out. Early, for a change. Her heart felt like a stone in her chest.

She pulled the curtain shut and picked up Gabby from the nubby kitchen rug the pup had claimed as her own. "I need a snuggle," she whispered, and the puppy nuzzled against her neck as if she understood.

This time, Meg acknowledged, she should have been the one to make the first move toward reconciliation. She should have gone to Rio to explain. He'd have understood. He might have been angry with her initially, but he would have understood.

And forgiven her.

Go to bed, she told herself. But she was despondent. Nothing would be different tomorrow. Not the next day, or the next.

She wasn't pregnant and she'd never hold a child of her own.

At a knock on the back door, Meg's gut seized. The day's upheavals had exhausted her. She wasn't sure if she was up to giving Rio the explanation he deserved.

Just try. This time, don't run away.

She opened the door, still holding the sleeping puppy against her shoulder. Rather like the baby she'd once been afraid of, then, much later, longed for with all her heart.

Rio loomed out of the dark. "I thought I should check on you."

"I feel okay. My head is sore, but the headache's almost gone." She moved deeper into the kitchen. "Come in."

He closed the door behind him but didn't enter any farther. There was a remoteness about him that reminded her of when he'd first arrived.

Another hard lesson. She never really appreciated what she had until it was gone.

"Want to talk?" she asked.

"Will you?"

"It's another thing I owe you."

"You didn't think so earlier."

She tucked her hair behind her ears. His skepticism pricked at her, but she was determined to keep cool. That was the only way she could get through this.

"You took me by surprise."

"I could say the same." He removed his jacket and hung it on the hook, then faced her with his arms crossed over his chest. His black hair gleamed under the kitchen fluorescents. Suddenly she wanted to be in his arms, feeling the cadence of his heart and the steadiness of his breath. When they were close, she wasn't so afraid.

"Meg," he said. "What's going on with you?" His concern was genuine. "You shouldn't have been riding Axx in such an emotional state."

"Of course not." Gabby whimpered against Meg's neck. "But I wasn't thinking."

After seeing the ironically incisive "minus" mark on the test stick, she'd plunged into one of the dark moods she'd thought she'd escaped by returning to the ranch and starting over. But the fall off the mustang had knocked the blinders off her. She'd been foolish to think her problems wouldn't follow her. They always had before, no matter how fast she ran.

Meg walked into the living room and put the puppy on a corner of the couch.

Rio followed. "She's tuckered out."

Meg exhaled. "So'm I."

He looked at her so directly, so intently, that she was uncomfortable for a few seconds until she realized he was checking her eyes again, not trying to draw her into an embrace. Next he'd be asking her to follow his moving finger.

"Your face is pink."

She shrugged. He'd made her blush and he had no idea. Why she should be feeling this physical attraction. Now of all times, was a mystery to her.

Except that she'd never felt so naked before.

So that was why they called it baring your soul.

"Let's get this over with." She switched on a lamp, then circled the room, too nervous to sit, ending up at the picture window. A truck drove by on the main road, going so slowly she thought for a moment that it was going to turn into her driveway.

"Just tell me why you lied to me," Rio said.

She rubbed her forehead. The motion pulled her scalp over the tender bump on the back of her head. She resisted touching it.

Oh, God. This was going to be horrible.

"I didn't lie, exactly."

"Then how did you lie—imprecisely?" He winced. "Sorry. It's not the time for sarcasm."

She took another deep breath. "The truth is, there's a small possibility, a very small possibility, that I could get pregnant. But no chance at all of carrying a baby to term."

He said only, "You should have told me that before we slept together."

"Yeah."

"I realize that you're not big on exposing your personal issues."

Or baring her soul. She'd told him so little, owed him

so much, yet still she couldn't give up everything. She couldn't stand to see the hurt the truth would cause him.

He cleared his throat. "You can't have a baby?"

"No."

"I'm sorry. Do you…want one?"

She glanced at his face. Was he hopeful? Did he want her to want a baby?

"I did," she admitted. "I became pregnant when I was with Jase."

"Ah. So that's what you meant by never getting pregnant again. I wondered."

She rushed on, the better to avoid the entire explanation. "The pregnancy was unexpected, but I was happy about it after I got used to the idea. But then—well, things didn't work out the way I'd hoped. Our relationship fell apart." Her knees went weak and she sat abruptly. Gabby stirred, making a puppy moan in her sleep.

"I had a miscarriage. It wasn't—wasn't the first time." Her claustrophobia threatened to overwhelm her. She needed to run. "That was about a month before I came back to Wild River. I was—" She gulped, clutching at the couch cushions to hold herself down. "I was finished."

Rio sat beside her and held her hand. "You're not finished, Meg."

Her hand twisted in his. She closed her eyes, not willing to debate the point. "I guess I should have explained before. It was just easier not to." She sent him a pleading look. "I didn't plan to mislead you, but then I didn't plan to have sex with you either."

"Twice." His thumb rubbed against the heel of her palm. "And the next time?"

She blinked. "Aren't you angry with me?"

"I'm confused. The test you took. I'm assuming it was negative."

"Yes. Negative."

"But you said you were upset when you took Axxaashe out. Why would you be upset if you're not pregnant?"

Trapped. She pulled her hand out of his.

"Did you want to be pregnant, Meg? With my baby?"

"Good God, no. Why would I? Do you think I actually want to go through that trauma again?"

Rio looked at her intently. "Again?"

She almost bit her tongue. "I meant after losing Jase's baby."

"Maybe you were hoping that this time…"

Ah, there it was. Hope. Hoping against hope.

She shot up from the couch. She didn't want to hope. But she couldn't help it.

"There's no use," she said despairingly.

She faced Rio, her stomach churning. "I can't ever have a baby. So don't bother looking at me like that."

Warmth, understanding, forgiveness, love—it all spilled out of his eyes like twin lanterns shining out of the darkness. And she had to turn away.

She looked down at her shaking hands. Traced the indelible scars. "Don't, Rio. We won't ever be a family."

She wanted to run more than ever, but something held her to the floor. Something made her stay.

Rio put his arms around her. She sank into the embrace with a deep sigh.

He whispered against her ear. "There are all kinds of families, Meggie Jo."

A STRANGE LIGHT showed through the half-drawn curtains. A flickering against the night. Northern lights, Meg thought with a sleep-blurred mind as she closed her eyes and burrowed against Rio's strong smooth shoulders.

He made a murmuring sound and reached back to pat her hip. "It's not time to get up."

A minute later, Meg lifted her head. It wasn't even dawn. But that light….

She sniffed. A faint acrid odor hung in the air.

She bolted upright, clutching at Rio's arm. "Wake up. I think there's a fire." She scrambled out of bed. "Oh my God. The barn. The horses."

They threw on some clothes and burst out of the house into the cold air. Flames licked at the side of the bunkhouse.

"I'll check the barn," Rio said as he pulled on the jacket she handed him. An old grease-stained canvas coat of her father's. "You go back inside and phone the fire department."

"But the horses—"

"Don't worry. The fire won't spread over the frozen ground that fast. It's not even that bad. I can probably put it out with a hose." He gave her a push back inside. "Go on. Put on more clothes."

Meg called 911 and returned to the bedroom to slip into a pair of jeans and a warm sweatshirt. She ran out to the barn, where Rio had turned on all the lights. "No sign of trouble," he called over the clamor of the agitated horses, whinnying as they moved restlessly around their stalls. "They're just nervous."

"I'll get the hose." She lifted down the heavy loops of the long water hose and threw it onto the floor of the aisle. Rio grabbed one end and screwed it into the spigot while she uncoiled hastily, the stiff cold rubber slithering through her bare hands. The hose snaked around her, almost tripping her up as she found the nozzle end and dragged it through the doorway.

The flames had reached the eaves along the eastern side of the bunkhouse, forming a thin sheet of fire over the log wall. She panted desperately, wrenching the muscles in her shoulders as she stumbled over the frozen ground with the heavy hose.

Suddenly Rio was beside her. "Let me."

He pulled the hose the last several feet and aimed a stream of water at the fire.

Meg stood back, the cold air catching short in her lungs. Her brain spun with questions. The fire made no sense. How had it started on the outside of the cabin—in October—in the cold?

Arson? Why?

"Your book!" she shouted to Rio.

He waved her off.

"Your book," she repeated, thinking he hadn't heard. "You have to rescue it."

When still he didn't move, she did. His book was important. Vital. It was his future. She dashed toward the cabin.

"Meg, no!" he shouted.

She pressed her hand over her mouth and stepped through the smoky veil that hung across the door. Inside, the bunkhouse was filled with the flickering orange light that had awakened her. The shifting smoke and murky shapes caused a moment of disorientation before her head cleared. She knew exactly where she was.

"Meg!" Rio shouted from behind her.

She grabbed the laptop off the desk and bolted toward his voice, colliding with him halfway across the room. He wrapped his arms around her and together they staggered outside, coughing violently.

He inhaled. "That was a stupid thing to do."

Water sprayed in an arc from the hose he'd flung aside. Meg pressed the laptop to her abdomen to protect it as she hacked to clear her lungs. "No, it was important. Very important." Her voice was hoarse and her throat felt raw from the smoke she'd swallowed, but she had to say it anyway. "Rio, you're going to publish this book."

BY MORNING, Meg was well and truly done in. The Treetop Volunteer Fire Department had come and gone, after putting out the last of the flames and consuming multiple pots of coffee and every sweet roll, biscuit and piece of toast in the house. The horses had settled down and were contentedly munching on their morning ration of alfalfa. The puppy was sprawled in a deep sleep on the kitchen rug, her whiskers twitching.

Rio and his mother were on cleanup duty, inside and outside. They'd ordered Meg back to bed, but she hadn't been able to sleep, even after a long hot soapy shower had removed the stink of smoke from her skin and hair. She'd dressed and was just about to switch on the blow-dryer when she heard Rio return to the kitchen.

She pulled her damp hair back in a ponytail and went to talk to him about the fire.

His low voice stopped her in the hallway. "The chief said the accelerant was gasoline."

She stood outside the kitchen door in her stocking feet. That the fire had been deliberately set was no surprise. The jump from petty vandalism to arson was more alarming.

Arson and malicious destruction of property, she corrected herself, thinking of Rio's writing. Among the clamor of activity when the fire truck had arrived with sirens blaring, he'd taken the laptop from her with the gentle explanation that all of his material was backed up and stored online. The book had never been in danger. But he'd given her a quick hug anyway, and whispered a thank-you in her ear.

"You could have been killed, Rio," Virginia was saying. She sounded nearly as strung out as Meg felt.

"I doubt that was the plan. The door to the bunkhouse wasn't locked. Whoever set the fire probably knew I wasn't inside."

Meg put out a hand to push through the swinging door, but stopped when she heard Virginia say, "You were sleeping here? At the ranch house."

"That's right." There was a long pause, filled only with the sound of Rio's mother washing something at the sink.

Finally he said, "I'm still hoping to make it work with Meg."

She caught her breath, not understanding his capacity for forgiveness. How could he keep wanting her when she'd hurt him over and over again? How could he continue taking the risk of loving her? She couldn't even love herself.

And he won't either, once he finally learns what you've been keeping from him for the past ten years.

"I was afraid of that." Virginia sounded resigned. "You know what will happen. What's happening right this minute. Look at the uproar she's already caused."

Rio laughed in disbelief. "Meg's not causing the trouble."

"I suppose not. But she's the catalyst."

"I don't see it that way."

Meg steeled herself. "Someone's after one of us,"

she announced, stepping into the kitchen. "They've got it in for either me or Rio. Maybe both."

Virginia had finished scrubbing the coffeepot and moved on to disinfecting the countertops. She gave Meg a spare glance, her mouth pulled taut.

Rio sat at the table, still wearing the clothes he'd fought the fire in—jeans and a T-shirt, both smudged with smoke and dirt. His muddy boots had been kicked off at the back door. "You could be right," he said with a tired shrug, "but what's the point? Rocks, a dented mailbox— that's nothing. Even the fire wasn't very serious."

"Could've been," Meg said, taking her usual chair across from Rio.

He shook his head. "They knew you were home to catch it before it spread."

"Maybe this was about your memoir. They might have thought they were destroying it. Or at least putting a scare into you."

Virginia froze for a second, then resumed her vigorous scrubbing.

"Mrs. Carefoot," Meg said, "please sit down with us. You've done enough."

The woman had arrived as soon as the news of the fire had reached the Stone ranch. After ascertaining that Rio was safe, she'd scoured the kitchen cupboards for ingredients and mixes and gone to work, turning out the cinnamon rolls and other provisions that had fed the firefighters.

Rio stood to hold out a chair. His mother hesitated

before sitting with a sigh, placing her well-worn hands on the tabletop. Her expression was unreadable.

Meg took a breath. "Tell us what you know."

Virginia acknowledged the request with a nod. She didn't speak.

"What?" Rio said, frowning.

"Just a minute." Meg hurried into her father's study. Ever since the quilt show, her mind had been turning over several possible scenarios. She'd been certain that she'd seen the Peak Properties logo before. If she could just remember where.

The answer had finally come while she was in the shower. The logo had been on a letterhead among her father's papers.

She returned from the office, the letter crumpled in her hand. "Billy's company was trying to buy Wild River. He made an extremely generous offer for the ranch, but Dad refused."

She stopped, suddenly fixed by the belated realization that her father had refused—and what that meant.

He hadn't sold out. He hadn't changed his will. Even though his cold nature and sheer mulish pride had kept them from a deathbed reunion, he'd still wanted his daughter to have the ranch.

Which was probably as close as Richard Lennox had ever come to showing Meg he cared.

"What does that have to do with the fire?" Rio asked.

Meg collapsed into the chair. She studied the letter for a minute, trying to collect herself. "Uh, maybe nothing. Unless Billy—or someone—is trying to make me feel unwanted so that I'll sell out."

Rio wasn't persuaded. "Think about it, Meg. Can you imagine Billy smashing a mailbox? That's more Mitch Vaughn's speed."

"Exactly. Billy hired a lackey." Meg was covertly watching Virginia, whose gaze seemed stuck on the plain gold band she wore on her right ring finger. Billy's name had brought no reaction.

"That's possible," Rio said. "The fire was definitely arson."

Meg cocked her head. "How does the cabin look?"

"Not so bad. One side is blackened and there's some damage to the roof. But the fire didn't penetrate very deeply into the logs. They can be sanded and revarnished."

"What about the interior?"

"Minimal smoke damage."

"There'll be an investigation. One of the deputies was already asking me about motives." Meg gave a rueful shrug. "I told him that I may not have any friends here, but I couldn't think of any enemies either. I didn't mention the Vaughns' nephew."

"Why not?"

"Didn't feel right. We only have suspicions. No proof." Meg coughed at the tickle in her throat. "I'm familiar with what it's like to be the object of suspicion."

"But not wrongly convicted," Virginia said with bite.

Rio raised a hand. "Hold off, Ma. I wasn't actually convicted."

"Thanks to Mr. Stone."

Meg's hopes of a breakthrough faded. Virginia would always defend Stone, even if that also meant defending Billy over her own son.

"Right," Rio said. "How could I forget? It was real big of him to clean up the mess."

"The point is," Meg said, "that Billy's buying up land. Didn't the Vaughns say they'd received an offer, too?"

Rio nodded. "They're considering it."

"I saw Billy at the quilt show. He's still interested."

Rio looked askance. "In you?"

Meg smiled. "In the ranch."

He seemed vaguely abashed. Meg could feel herself coloring at she thought of him telling his mother that he hadn't given up on her.

"What about—" Rio's brow furrowed. "So, let's say that Billy really wants to buy your land. Why should he try to run you off before you've even refused an offer?" He reconsidered. "Or did you?"

"He didn't give me the chance." She grimaced, thinking it over. "I guess you're right. There's not a lot of motive for our vandal to be Billy. Unless your mother has something to add?" Meg looked at the woman. "I think maybe she does."

Please.

"Yes," Virginia said with gravity. Her hands twisted against each other until her fingers were tangled.

Rio laid his hand on her arm encouragingly.

His mother pulled off her ring and set it on the table. "Billy's not to blame for your troubles," she said with an air of finality. "But William is."

CHAPTER FIFTEEN

RIO STARED at the ring. He couldn't remember for sure when his mother had begun wearing it. He must have been a child.

After he'd learned that Stone was his father, the ring had seemed like a glaringly obvious piece of evidence to him, but none of the Stone family had ever seemed to notice. And his mother had never explained it. At times, he'd told himself that maybe he was wrong and the ring hadn't been a gift from Stone at all. But in his heart, he'd been certain. And he'd resented it.

Seeing Virginia take off the ring wasn't as big a relief as he'd imagined.

"Stone's behind this?" Meg asked. Her eyes sought Rio's. "How do you know?"

"I'm the housekeeper. I hear them talking, I see who visits. I clean up after their meetings."

Rio stared at the ring, waiting for her to continue. There had to be more, if she felt that she was betraying Stone to such a degree that she could no longer wear his ring.

"Last week, Mitch Vaughn came to the house unexpectedly, asking for payment on a job. William wasn't happy about that. He rushed Vaughn out through the kitchen." Virginia tipped her head toward Rio. "You see, after you first told me about Vaughn's belligerence toward you and Meg, I began to pay closer attention. Then a few days ago, I overheard an odd telephone call. I couldn't tell what it meant, but I knew that it was about another job for Vaughn."

"You're saying that Stone set up the fire." Rio slowly shook his head. "Why didn't you warn us?"

"I wasn't certain." Virginia looked pained, conflicted. "Besides, I doubt William intended for you to be hurt."

"Don't defend him."

She lowered her eyes. "I'm not. It's the truth. He only wanted the book stopped. The other incidents—I think those were just Vaughn's idea of revenge. I accused William, but he passed them off. He said if they bothered Meg enough to make her want to sell to Billy, then so be it."

Rio felt singed. "Still. Whatever twisted loyalty you have to him, you should have told me sooner."

"That was wrong—keeping it from you. There's no excuse, only a poor reason. I was worried about you two becoming involved again. That you'd find yourself in trouble, defending Meg. And then, one way or another, I'd lose you." Virginia put her face in her hands, catching a sob. "I'm sorry."

Rio wasn't sure how to respond. His mother was finally choosing to put him above her relationship with Stone, but there was no triumph in that. No great, sudden release of frustration. There'd been too many years of feeling unworthy and unwanted.

Or, maybe, he'd already dealt with those issues and had simply moved on. The satisfaction of an acknowledgment, even some sort of revenge, wasn't necessary.

He looked at Meg, who'd been silent. Her face was stark, her narrow nose and sharp bone structure more prominent than ever with her hair pulled tightly back.

"I can't blame you for being worried about me and Rio," she said to Virginia. "I've felt that way myself. I haven't always been good for him. Never as good as he's been for me."

Rio frowned. "I didn't expect you to be good for me, Meg."

"But my—others did. Maybe I did, too. I could have tried harder, at least."

She rubbed the back of her neck. He wanted to comfort her, but even though she'd showed signs of softening, being more willing to meet him partway, she still didn't trust him.

He addressed his mother instead. "Will you tell the sheriff about Stone's association with Vaughn?"

The lines in her face deepened. "I will if I have to. But is it necessary?"

He lifted his shoulders. "I'm not sure. What do you think, Meg?"

She hesitated, searching his face, probably reading the conflict there. Punishment for the man who'd rejected him versus one last gesture of appeasement.

"Don't do it for my sake," she said. "There's been no major damage done, as long as it's made clear that the dirty tricks must stop."

Virginia exhaled. "I'll tell William that the game is up." She glanced at Rio. "We'll talk when I turn in my resignation. It's time I retired, don't you think?"

"If that's what you want," he said, nodding reassuringly. She'd made a hard choice, one he appreciated. Even if he no longer needed to see his biological father brought down, he could admit that there was some satisfaction in knowing that Stone would lose the heart of his home. And that the man probably wouldn't realize it until it was too late.

THE NEXT DAY, Rio drove through the tall spire gates of the Stone ranch. He'd sworn that he wouldn't return without an invitation from Stone himself. But everything had changed. His mother had tendered her resignation that morning. Stone, full of false umbrage over the accusations, had ordered her off the ranch immediately, then abruptly departed for the family home on the East Coast where his wife was for the winter.

The lion that had once seemed so mighty had turned into a mouse and scurried away at the first threat.

Rio's hands tightened on the wheel. The ranch looked the same as he remembered from ten years ago. The main house was a white columned palace with brick trim and a vast slate roof. White board fences stretched in all directions. The barren trees and bushes bound in twine and orange webbing added to the air of desolation. The only outdoor activity was around the distant barns, where a few horses and cattle dotted the paddocks.

Rio parked his rusty old pickup at the side entrance, adjacent to the long six-car garage. Feeling like a stranger, he knocked at the side door. As a boy he'd flown in and out of the house, all about the day's adventures with Meg, the discoveries and campfires and horseback trips into the mountains. Thanks to her, it hadn't been such a lousy life after all, playing the odd man out at Stone Ranch.

His mother opened the door and gave him a fast hug. He looked into her face, but there was no sign of turmoil. Not even tear tracks. Her calm was almost eerie. Certainly disturbing, considering she was about to leave her longtime home.

"How are you doing?" he asked.

"I'm ready to go."

"You're ready? That was fast."

"There wasn't that much to pack."

She led Rio into the large, well-appointed kitchen that had been as close to a home here as he'd known. It, too, was clean and white and sterile, from the bleached oak floor to the banks of tall cabinets. Bins and baskets of produce added punches of color—red potatoes, bulbous purple eggplants, yellow peppers and deep orange tangerines. Virginia's herb garden still grew in small clay pots in a greenhouse window, but her woven wall hangings had been removed. The sweater from the back of one of the chairs. Her dispenser of hand lotion by the sink. The family photos she'd stuck to the stainless-steel refrigerator.

Lissy sat at the center island, dabbing at her eyes with a tissue. "I can't believe you're leaving, Mrs. Carefoot. It's just plain wrong. You're not old enough to retire."

"Oh, I suppose I'll find something to keep me busy. There's my friend Marian, who runs the quilting store in town. She's always looking for help."

"But you're so good at taking care of us," Lissy wailed, before cutting herself short. She laughed. "I must sound like a big baby."

Virginia patted her shoulder.

Lissy dropped the tissue and tore into a blueberry muffin, popping piece after piece into her mouth. "Hi, Rio," she said, glumly chewing. "Where are you taking your mom?"

"To Meg's." She'd offered her extra bedroom and, surprisingly, his mother had accepted rather than going to stay with family in Montana or friends in Treetop.

"Well, that'll be close quarters for the three of you," Lissy said. "Her house is so small and dark. It'll be a long winter."

"I won't overstay my welcome," Virginia said. "I plan to look for a small apartment in town. As long as Rio's staying, that is. He's barely been back and I haven't spent enough time with him."

"I'm staying," he said. Oh, yeah, he was staying.

Lissy ripped off another piece of muffin. "Even if you sell the book?"

"Even then."

"Because of Meg, huh?"

"She's my girl," he said simply. She always had been. Even when she'd ended their romance and gone off with other boys, she'd always come back to him. Except the last time, the night of the fire.

"Well, I'm sorry about my dad, anyway, how he's been trying to stop you from getting the book published. He's just so self-centered. He believes the world should revolve around him." Lissy laughed shrilly. "Doesn't he get that it revolves around me?"

No one else laughed at the awkward joke. Rio followed his mother into her small suite, comprising a modest bedroom and sitting room. She pointed out what she was taking with her—a small amount of furnishings, several boxes of books and knickknacks, clothing. Everything would fit into the back of his pickup. A sad commentary.

"Are you sure you're okay?" he asked, making the last of the trips back and forth. His mother was stuffing bed pillows into a trash bag. The bed had been stripped.

"I'm fine."

"This is a big change. It's all right to be emotional. You don't have to hold back on my account."

Virginia sat on the edge of the mattress. "I have to confess, this is not as major a move as you might believe. William and I haven't been close for a very long time."

Rio couldn't speak.

"Not since you went away," she continued. "I'd asked him to save you, but then I couldn't forgive him for the way he did it. I had hoped he would finally show you that he did love you, in his way. But instead he got rid of you."

"It wasn't—"

"No. It was his fault. Maybe you weren't forced into anything, but you didn't have much choice either." Virginia hesitated. When she opened her mouth, Rio thought she might add Meg's name to the blame list, but instead she let out a choked sob.

"And it's my fault. Raising you here seemed like the thing to do, but it was a mistake. If only I'd taken you and started over somewhere else, we could have had a home of our own. Maybe then we would have been a real family instead of—of—" She pressed her hands against her face.

Rio sat and put his arms around her. "You were a good mother. Living on the ranch wasn't so bad. I had everything I needed." Almost everything. "And there was Meg."

His mother dragged in a breath. She must have got back some of her grit, because the look she aimed at him said that getting him away from Meg might not have been such a bad thing. She would take some convincing on that point, but her stay at Wild River Ranch was a good start.

He gave her a squeeze. "Let's finish up."

"There's not much left to do." Virginia walked to the door, wiping the last of the tears from her face. She paused with her hand on the knob. "Only a last look around the kitchen. Poor Lissy is having a hard time."

"She's losing a mother. You made Billy and Lissy a home here." True enough. Rio's half siblings had craved their father's approval and acceptance just as much as he had. They'd all been left wanting.

Virginia walked out wearing a sad smile. Rio looked around the room, stripped of the comfort and warmth his mother had instilled in her quiet way.

From his jeans pocket he took the ring she'd left on Meg's kitchen table. He held it in his palm for a minute, waiting for it to be more than a ring. A symbol of a family unmade, of a life half lived.

But that didn't happen. The ring was just a ring.

Rio placed it on the bureau and went out to the kitchen to tell Lissy goodbye.

Billy was there, bluff in his fine western-cut suit and broad smile. "Rio, my man. I hear we're losing your mother."

He accepted Billy's handshake. "About time, I think."

Billy gave Virginia a bear hug. "We'll sure miss you, Mrs. C. And your home-cooked meals."

She smiled, still susceptible to the Stone brand of flattery. "I won't be far."

Billy turned sober as they walked to Rio's pickup and loaded the last few items in the back. "I hope that someday you'll both be able to forgive my father. If I'd realized sooner…"

About the vandalism, Rio assumed. Not the bigger transgression.

"William always was too grandiose for his own good." Virginia's gaze swept over the house. She gave a quiet sigh and climbed into Rio's truck.

"And you?" Billy's face was blotched with color, but he looked Rio in the eye. "Will you be able to forgive my—our father?"

Our father. A shocking admission, and one that sounded all wrong to Rio's ears.

He shook his head. "He's not my father. He forfeited that right a long time ago."

"I get you." Billy shrugged. "Can't blame you for holding a grudge."

"But not against us!" Lissy stepped up beside her brother. She clasped Rio's right hand and wrist. "Please say that you won't reject us, too. You might not need William Walker Stone as a father, but you can still have a brother and sister." She gave his arm a shake. "Never mind Dad. We want to be your family."

Rio frowned. Although Lissy seemed genuine, he couldn't read Billy through the guy's polished facade. He asked roughly, "You feel that way?" Seriously doubting it.

"I'd like to start out as friends. Then we might eventually become brothers." Billy rubbed his jaw, suddenly seeming more like the awkward boy he'd once been. "I admit to being jealous of you as a kid. I was only a year younger, but I always felt like the chubby tagalong, half a step behind, never catching up. No good at riding or baseball or climbing trees. And it sure didn't help having Meg calling me Baby Billy."

"Huh," Rio said.

Lissy scowled. "Meg wanted Rio to herself."

"That was mutual."

"Yeah." Billy grinned. "You two were quite a pair. Is she still as possessive?"

Needy, Rio thought. She needed what he needed—a family.

"She's too independent minded to admit to it," he said, bemused. "But she has acquired a few additions to the household in spite of herself. A mustang mare and foal. A puppy from the Vaughns."

"And now you and your mother, too," Lissy said with a girlish pout. "She'd better learn to share. Because we're not giving you up so easily this time. Right, Billy?"

Billy cuffed Rio's shoulder. "Right."

Lissy kissed his cheek. "That settles it. You're going to be our brother, Rio Carefoot. Get used to it."

They'd already lost so many years, but that didn't seem to matter so much anymore. And while Billy and Lissy weren't the easiest people to get along with, that somehow made them seem almost like real siblings. Despite the rivalry and mistrust, the three of them truly shared a bond.

"Okay." Rio swallowed the lump in his throat. "I guess maybe I can do that."

CHAPTER SIXTEEN

MEG HAD RETREATED TO the barn after seeing Virginia settled up at the ranch house. It had been so long since there was another woman around the place she'd felt awkward and strange in her own home.

"Finally we have a mother," Meg told Axxaashe. She leaned over the bottom half of the Dutch door to stroke the mustang's shoulder. "Other than you, that is."

Except that Axxaashe no longer had her colt. She'd lost him. Granted, that had been the natural manner of these things.

Meg sighed, tired of beating herself up.

The sound of a door slamming at the house got her moving. She left the mustang's would-be stall and climbed the wooden ladder to the haymow, which was open at the center to allow bales to be thrown down into the barn's aisle.

"Bombs away," she called, hearing Rio's footsteps as she tossed the first bale. It hit hard and broke apart, scattering across the floor.

"Hold it, Meg." He appeared below her, looking up. "Want to come down from there? I've got news."

Her heart jumped to her throat. He sounded…satisfied. Complete. She'd never given him that. Or felt it herself.

"You come up," she called. "I've got to shift these bales around."

The rungs creaked as he climbed. Meg remembered how they'd scrambled up the ladder as kids, completely carefree and oblivious to danger. She had once dropped a rope through the opening to use as a swing, a pastime soon halted by her father when he'd come upon the mess they'd made, tossing bales down to make a soft place to land. Rio's idea. She hadn't spared a moment's thought to falling. If anything, she'd have counted on Rio standing by to catch her. She'd always counted on him being there for her.

But then you didn't give him the chance, the one time you really should have.

Meg dropped onto a bale as Rio's head and shoulders appeared above the loft floor. He paused there, arms propped on the floorboards. "Look at you. Hay in your hair and muck on your boots and still you're beautiful."

She brushed herself off. He made her feel beautiful, even when she wasn't. "You need glasses."

"Nope. You're beautiful. You always were." Rio climbed the rest of the way into the haymow, limber and narrow hipped in his jacket and jeans. He dropped his chin, studying her for a moment before a slow smile spread across his face. His eyes were lit with a unique happiness. "Meg. I sold the book."

"What?" She'd almost forgotten that a deal was pending.

"My agent just called. There's an offer—a good offer. Not as great as it might have been, considering, but still good enough. There are details to work out yet, but I'm pretty sure I'll be taking the deal."

She was glad she'd already sat. "Congratulations."

"Is that all you have to say?"

She took a breath. "Really—congratulations. That's great news. I'm sure the book will be a success."

She stood and began tossing bales again, in no logical manner. One split apart into flakes.

Rio stepped over the jumbled pile. "Are you thinking of seeing yourself in print?"

Meg hefted another bale, breathing hard. "I'll get used to it."

"You won't have to."

She stopped, the heavy bale still clutched to her chest. The wires that bound the hay bit into her hands through her leather gloves. "What do you mean?"

"I called my agent a few days ago and told her that I wanted to write the book without naming names. She said we'd get less of an advance, but I don't care." He paused, waiting for her to say something, but she was too overwhelmed. "I, uh, realize that not being named won't necessarily mean all that much to you or my mother locally, since everyone in Treetop already knows who you are, but you will be spared the wider exposure."

Yes, the townspeople know who we are, Meg thought. And what we've done. But then, they always had. Whatever wrongs had been done, that hadn't made any difference to the people who knew them best. Those with the generosity to accept the good with the bad.

Like Rio himself.

"Maybe it's cold comfort, but at least your names won't become completely public," he concluded.

"Oh," she said, trying to process it. She rested the bale on its narrow end and pulled off her gloves. "Stone will be pleased about that."

"That's not why I did it." Rio shrugged. "But seeing him embarrassed didn't hold much appeal to me when it came right down to it. Definitely not worth hurting my mother, or you."

"But I told you I was fine with it."

"Well, I'm not." He stepped closer, within arm's distance. The dusty light seemed to part around him, swirling with the golden flecks of chaff. "Did you think I wanted to punish you, Meg?"

"I was rotten to you." Her voice came out weak. She didn't like that but there seemed to be nothing she could do about it. "I was careless with you. I should have—" She searched for the words. "I wished I'd valued you more. Believed in you."

His brow furrowed. "Believed in us, you mean."

"No. I should have believed in you."

"Are you talking about then—or now?"

"Then," she blurted.

"Then," he echoed. "Like the night you ran away." He spread his hands, reaching toward her. "What about it?"

"I don't know. It's done. Why bother—" She cut herself off and bolted past him, heading for the ladder. He tried to catch her by the arm, but she was elusive, ducking and slipping by the way she used to when they'd played tag. Played catch-me-if-you-can. Played at lovemaking.

Rio followed her down into the barn. She grabbed one of the bales that had already split and went to Caprice's stall, shaking the flake of alfalfa apart as she stuffed it into the hay net.

He stood at the stall door. "What happened that night, Meg?"

She didn't look at him. "The usual. I had a big fight with my dad. You know."

"Maybe I don't. What was the fight about?"

Her voice dropped to a rough whisper. "He said I was a stupid slut and that I should leave the ranch for good. Nice, huh?" Her eyes welled. "I'm not sure why I cared. I wanted to leave."

Rio inhaled. "Damn, Meg. I wish you'd told me that he was so cruel to you."

"He wasn't, normally. But that night…" Her emotions were huge inside her, pushing against her ribs, her throat. "I'd told him that I was pregnant."

Rio didn't speak. She held her breath until the silence and the tension were too much for her to bear and then she burst out at him, almost angrily even though she blamed no one but herself. "Did you hear me, Rio? I said I was pregnant."

"Whose baby?"

She spun around. He stood outside the box stall, staring. His eyes were almost black, forming deep hollows above his slanted cheekbones.

"Yours."

"Mine. You're sure?"

"Yes, I might have been a stupid slut, but I knew who the baby's father was."

Rio winced. "What happened to it?"

"I had a miscarriage a few days later. That was when Kris dumped me. After the bleeding started and wouldn't stop, he dropped me off at a dinky hospital in some godforsaken town in Nevada and took off like a bat out of hell. He didn't want to be involved." She bumped Rio with the door as she opened and then closed it behind her.

He went to the feed bins as if he were sleepwalking and began scooping out portions of grain. "Why didn't you tell me, that night in the Vaughns' barn?"

"I wanted to. But I was afraid you'd stop me from leaving town. You'd put your arms around me and tell me everything would be all right. But where could I have gone? What was I going to do with a baby? My father didn't want me on the ranch. You were going off to college in the fall—"

"I would have figured something out."

All the uncertain anger and blame had drained out of

her. "Yes. You would have. You would have given up your shot at college, probably. Got a crummy job instead. And that was almost as bad to me as the thought of getting stuck in Treetop, a mother at the age of eighteen. Both our lives over before they'd barely begun."

"They wouldn't have been over. Things would've been tough, but we might have been happy."

If she'd given them the chance, Meg thought.

"You might have," she said. "I don't think I would. I didn't want to be pregnant. I wasn't ready to settle down, even with you."

"So you're saying that ultimately you were glad that you had a miscarriage."

"God, no!" With a searing immediacy, she remembered how frightened and alone she'd been. And how wounded by the loss, even though she hadn't been ready for a baby. "Just because I didn't want to be pregnant right then didn't mean I wouldn't have loved the baby anyway. Even if that meant loving it enough to give it up for adoption."

Not thinking, Rio dumped grain into the bowl in Axxaashe's stall. "Is that what you would have done?"

"Maybe. I don't know."

He dropped the scoop to scrape back his hair with a shaking hand. "You should have told me, Meg."

His sorrow was breaking her heart. "Yes." Impulsively, she went to him, leaned her forehead against his arm. "I was stubborn and selfish."

He turned and wound his arms around her, holding her arms down so she had no choice but to stand with him.

"I'm sorry," she whispered. "But believe me, I've been punished for my poor decision."

"Don't think that way."

"I can't have a baby, Rio. I can't have your baby." She clutched at the front of his jacket. "We won't ever be a family."

"We already are, Meg."

"Not a real one."

"There are all kinds of families, remember?"

"Yeah, sure." She tried to sound flippant, but it didn't work. There was too much feeling between them, feeling that had been there from the moment he'd stepped out of his truck and asked her for a job. Living with him, sleeping with him—that had only accelerated what was already between them.

She shook her head. "I want to give you a child of your own." To make up for her mistakes.

"Then we look into whatever treatments might help. If that doesn't work, we consider a surrogate. We adopt. Or, hell, we could choose to raise a lot of dogs and horses instead and be happy just being together."

She looked up at him with wonder. "How can you be so good to me when I've been so bad to you?"

He smiled.

"Please don't be nice. I'm so…so imperfect."

"And I'm not? C'mon, Meg. If I had an accident and was horribly scarred, or started drinking too much, or turned cranky as a bear in my old age, would you still love me anyway?"

"But—" She pushed at him a little with her fists. "That's not the same. I act like I'm tough, but inside I'm always afraid I'm fragile, like my mother." She crossed her hands at the wrist. Gulped. "I don't want to be your weakness, Rio."

He laughed in disbelief. "I can't even imagine that."

"Then *you* haven't been paying attention."

His hold on her loosened. One hand reached up to stroke her hair. "I've seen you vulnerable. You've shown me how much you need to feel loved. That's not the same thing as weakness."

"Feels like it."

"Then you haven't been paying attention."

She swallowed again. Tilted her face toward his. The hope she'd never been able to get rid of, no matter how hard she tried, renewed itself tenfold.

Rio's eyes were dark. Loving. He traced a finger along her cheek. "I admire you, Meggie Jo. You're strong. You're a survivor. I've loved you since the day we met, when you told me I looked like a scarecrow in my patched jeans. I love you today, even though you've made me sad and angry, too, for what we lost along the way. I'll love you tomorrow, and next month, and next year. You just have to trust that I'm telling you the truth." He touched his nose to hers and said in a husky voice, "Believe in us."

"I don't know how to do that."

"Are you sure? I think you just learned how." He nodded. "Up there in that haymow, when you finally told me what's been eating you up inside for the past ten years."

Meg wanted to believe that. She really did.

A movement in the box stall distracted her. The mustang mare had come inside, drawn by the irresistible scent of her evening grain. She stretched her head toward the feed bowl, nostrils fluttering.

One more step, Meg thought. *You can do it.*

Axxaashe lifted a hoof. A ripple went through her body as she put it down. After one last swing of her head to check out the strange surroundings, one more nervous flicker of her ears, she plunged her nose into the bowl and began to eat.

"Look at her," Meg whispered to Rio.

"She did it," he said, hugging Meg against his chest. "She came home."

Meg's heart swelled. "So did we."

Rio nodded. "For better or worse."

She looped her arms around his neck, completing the circuit that ran between them. A ring of flame. And a circle of rain.

Her eyes sought his. "I've always loved you."

"I knew that. I was only waiting for you to know it, too."

"I do," she said as his lips found hers with unerring accuracy. He had never wavered, not even once. "Finally, I really do."

* * * * *

*Rancher Ramsey Westmoreland's temporary cook
is way too attractive for his liking.
Little does he know Chloe Burton came to his
ranch with another agenda entirely....*

That man across the street had to be, without a doubt, the most handsome man she'd ever seen.

Chloe Burton's pulse beat rhythmically as he stopped to talk to another man in front of a feed store. He was tall, dark and every inch of sexy—from his Stetson to the well-worn leather boots on his feet. And from the way his jeans and Western shirt fit his broad muscular shoulders, it was quite obvious he had everything it took to separate the men from the boys. The combination was enough to corrupt any woman's mind and had her weakening even from a distance. Her body felt flushed. It was hot. Unsettled.

Over the past year the only male who had gotten her time and attention had been the e-mail. That was simply pathetic, especially since now she was practically drooling simply at the sight of a man. Even his stance—both hands in his jeans pockets, legs braced apart, was a pose she would carry to her dreams.

And he was smiling, evidently enjoying the conversation being exchanged. He had dimples, incredibly sexy dimples in not one but both cheeks.

"What are you staring at, Clo?"

Chloe nearly jumped. She'd forgotten she had a lunch date. She glanced over the table at her best friend from college, Lucia Conyers.

"Take a look at that man across the street in the blue shirt, Lucia. Will he not be perfect for Denver's first issue of *Simply Irresistible* or what?" Chloe asked with so much excitement she almost couldn't stand it.

She was the owner of *Simply Irresistible*, a magazine for today's up-and-coming woman. Their once-a-year Irresistible Man cover, which highlighted a man the magazine felt deserved the honor, had increased sales enough for Chloe to open a Denver office.

When Lucia didn't say anything but kept staring, Chloe's smile widened. "Well?"

Lucia glanced across the booth at her. "Since you asked, I'll tell you what I see. One of the Westmorelands—Ramsey Westmoreland. And yes, he'd be perfect for the cover, but he won't do it."

Chloe raised a brow. "He'd get paid for his services, of course."

Lucia laughed and shook her head. "Getting paid won't be the issue, Clo—Ramsey is one of the wealthiest sheep ranchers in this part of Colorado. But everyone knows what a private person he is. Trust me—he won't do it."

Chloe couldn't help but smile. The man was the epitome of what she was looking for in a magazine cover and she was determined that whatever it took, he would be it.

"Umm, I don't like that look on your face, Chloe. I've seen it before and know exactly what it means."

She watched as Ramsey Westmoreland entered the store with a swagger that made her almost breathless. She *would* be seeing him again.

Look for Silhouette Desire's
HOT WESTMORELAND NIGHTS
by Brenda Jackson,
available March 9 wherever books are sold.

Devastating, dark-hearted and...
looking for brides.

Look for

BOUGHT:
DESTITUTE YET DEFIANT

by *Sarah Morgan*
#2902

From the lowliest slums to Millionaire's Row...
these men have everything now but their brides—
and they'll settle for nothing less than the best!

Available March 2010
from Harlequin Presents!

Silhouette® **Desire**

THE WESTMORELANDS

NEW YORK TIMES
bestselling author

BRENDA JACKSON

HOT WESTMORELAND NIGHTS

Ramsey Westmoreland knew better than to lust after the hired help. But Chloe, the new cook, was just so delectable. Though their affair was growing steamier, Chloe's motives became suspicious. And when he learned Chloe was carrying his child this Westmoreland Rancher had to choose between pride or duty.

Available March 2010 wherever books are sold.

Always Powerful, Passionate and Provocative.

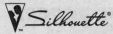

REQUEST YOUR FREE BOOKS!

2 FREE NOVELS PLUS 2 FREE GIFTS!

HARLEQUIN®

Super Romance®

Exciting, emotional, unexpected!

YES! Please send me 2 FREE Harlequin® Superromance® novels and my 2 FREE gifts (gifts are worth about $10). After receiving them, if I don't wish to receive any more books, I can return the shipping statement marked "cancel." If I don't cancel, I will receive 6 brand-new novels every month and be billed just $4.69 per book in the U.S. or $5.24 per book in Canada. That's a saving of close to 15% off the cover price! It's quite a bargain! Shipping and handling is just 50¢ per book in the U.S. and 75¢ per book in Canada.* I understand that accepting the 2 free books and gifts places me under no obligation to buy anything. I can always return a shipment and cancel at any time. Even if I never buy another book from Harlequin, the two free books and gifts are mine to keep forever.

135 HDN E4JC   336 HDN E4JN

Name _____ (PLEASE PRINT)

Address _____ Apt. #

City _____ State/Prov. _____ Zip/Postal Code

Signature (if under 18, a parent or guardian must sign)

Mail to the **Harlequin Reader Service:**
IN U.S.A.: P.O. Box 1867, Buffalo, NY 14240-1867
IN CANADA: P.O. Box 609, Fort Erie, Ontario L2A 5X3

Not valid for current subscribers to Harlequin Superromance books.

**Are you a current subscriber to Harlequin Superromance books and want to receive the larger-print edition?
Call 1-800-873-8635 today!**

* Terms and prices subject to change without notice. Prices do not include applicable taxes. N.Y. residents add applicable sales tax. Canadian residents will be charged applicable provincial taxes and GST. Offer not valid in Quebec. This offer is limited to one order per household. All orders subject to approval. Credit or debit balances in a customer's account(s) may be offset by any other outstanding balance owed by or to the customer. Please allow 4 to 6 weeks for delivery. Offer available while quantities last.

Your Privacy: Harlequin Books is committed to protecting your privacy. Our Privacy Policy is available online at www.eHarlequin.com or upon request from the Reader Service. From time to time we make our lists of customers available to reputable third parties who may have a product or service of interest to you. If you would prefer we not share your name and address, please check here. ☐

Help us get it right—We strive for accurate, respectful and relevant communications. To clarify or modify your communication preferences, visit us at www.ReaderService.com/consumerschoice.

HSR10

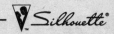

SPECIAL EDITION

FROM *USA TODAY* BESTSELLING AUTHOR
CHRISTINE RIMMER

A BRIDE FOR
JERICHO BRAVO

Marnie Jones had long ago buried her wild-child
impulses and opted to be "safe," romantically
speaking. But one look at born rebel Jericho Bravo
and she began to wonder if her thrill-seeking side
was about to be revived. Because if ever there was
a man worth taking a chance on, there he was,
right within her grasp....

*Available in March
wherever books are sold.*